EARL GRESHAM'S BRIDE

When heiress Kate Roscoe compromises herself through an innocent mistake, widower Earl Gresham steps in with an offer of marriage to save her reputation. She is soon deeply in love with him, but is beset by the problems of overseeing his grand household. The housekeeper is dishonest and the nanny of the earl's two children is heartless and lazy. But a far greater threat comes from his former mistress who will go to any lengths to destroy Kate's marriage.

ANGELA DRAKE

EARL GRESHAM'S BRIDE

Complete and Unabridged

LINFORD
Leicester

First published in Great Britain in 2011

First Linford Edition
published 2012

British Library CIP Data

Drake, Angela.
  Earl Gresham's bride. - -
(Linford romance library)
1. Love stories.
2. Large type books.
I. Title II. Series
823.9'2–dc23

ISBN 978–1–4448–0964–0

Published by
F. A. Thorpe (Publishing)
Anstey, Leicestershire

Set by Words & Graphics Ltd.
Anstey, Leicestershire
Printed and bound in Great Britain by
T. J. International Ltd., Padstow, Cornwall

This book is printed on acid-free paper

1

Kate Roscoe was sitting in the drawing room of the house her mother had rented for the London season of 1868, trying to read Emily Bronte's novel *Wuthering Heights* which she had found in the small but well-stocked library. But her mama's constant stream of remarks about ball gowns and the need to attract an aristocratic husband was impossible to ignore.

'Oyster satin with a rose pink underskirt,' Mrs Roscoe decided. 'How does that strike you, my dear?'

Kate closed her eyes briefly, thinking how lovely it would be to escape from the drawing room and take a walk in the park. Or maybe to slip away to the sanctuary of her bedroom and practise scales on her violin. There was little hope of either — not when Mama was running on at full steam.

'Kate?' Mrs Roscoe prompted, sharply.

Kate looked up from her book. 'I don't think rose pink suits me,' she said, trying to sound pleasant.

'But, my dear, it is all the fashion!' There was no point arguing with her mother in this mood.

Kate sighed. 'Very well, Mama.'

'Or maybe a soft sea green, with ivory beneath? That would suit your colouring.' Mrs Roscoe looked in despair at her daughter, whose hair was as red as a newly minted penny, her eyes a deep, tawny hazel. Very disappointing, when blonde hair and cornflower-blue eyes were so much more admired in London this season. Kate looked like a little girl from the North who loved to run wild over the moors. Which was, of course, the truth of the matter.

'That would be nice,' Kate said, but in a voice which told her mother she really could not care one way or another.

'The ball at Lady Follet's is very important, Kate.' Mrs Roscoe tone was serious to the point of severity. 'There

2

will be a great many eligible young men there — of high birth.'

'Yes, Mama. And I promise to be on my best behaviour.'

Mrs Roscoe found this less than convincing. 'You are almost twenty, Kate. It is high time you were married.' She reminded her daughter of this duty at least two or three times a day.

'Yes, Mama.' Kate bent her head to her book and grimaced into the pages. She had known for the past year, ever since her uncle had made her the sole beneficiary of his will, that she was a prize to be sought after by ambitious mothers eager to pair off their sons with a girl in possession of a considerable fortune — nine hundred and fifty thousand pounds, to be precise. According to her mother's advisor, the sum was increasing steadily, owing to the canniness of his investments on Kate's behalf. In addition, Kate's mother was wealthy in her own right, having been left the fortune her father had made from his mining company.

We are a family awash with money, she thought. *But has it made us happy? And how will I ever know that a man wishes to marry me for my own sake, rather than that of my wealth?*

She knew this was not a dilemma that concerned most of her mother's acquaintances — nor the young women she had met during the London season. Their view was that the more money one had, the better.

'Lord Walton will be there,' her mother continued. 'His father is a duke and cousin to the Queen.'

'Well then, he won't want someone like me — a little Northern girl from a family who have made their money from trade,' Kate remarked, immediately chiding herself — her mother was very sensitive on the issue of where her family's resources had sprung from.

Mrs Roscoe's face turned pink. 'I will not permit that kind of talk in our house,' she declared. 'The Roscoes have lived like aristocrats for two generations now.'

'Yes,' Kate agreed mildly. 'Anyway, Mama, at least trade is honourable. Most aristocrats obtained their money by robbing other people.'

Mrs Roscoe had to take some deep breaths. She could not understand where her daughter got her strange, rebellious ideas. She had heard that a number of modern young ladies were of the same turn of mind, but she personally had never met any. 'You read too many books,' she chided. 'And those terrible newspapers.'

'*The Times* and *The Observer* are very respectable publications,' Kate pointed out patiently.

'I order them for visiting gentlemen to read,' Mrs Roscoe retorted. 'They are not meant to entertain young ladies.' Tears came into her eyes.

'I'm sorry, Mama,' Kate said, getting up and kissing her parent's cheek. 'I didn't mean to upset you.' *Oh dear,* she thought. If only her mama knew it, Kate's reading the newspapers was the least she had to worry about.

Mrs Roscoe took out her handkerchief. 'No, dear — I know you don't really mean all those funny things you say.'

Kate gave a tiny grimace. 'And I shall be very polite to Lord Walton.'

'Oh, I'm so glad!' Mrs Roscoe began to brighten up at the marvellous prospect of Kate's eventually becoming a duchess.

Kate was privately reflecting that Lord Walton had the face of a fish and the brain of a bird; she had no intention of even allowing him to kiss her hand. She glanced out of the window, longing to go out and simply breathe in the fresh air, but she saw that her mother was still in a flutter. She sat down and touched her hand. 'I think I like the idea of a sea green gown.'

'Oh, dearest child!' Mrs Roscoe clapped her hands. 'Yes, that would be just the thing. We'll call for the carriage and go to Madame Antoinette's lovely shop in Bond Street right away to look for some fabrics.'

Kate smiled, reflecting that her situation was rather like that of a bird in a gilded cage. If she were to marry, would she simply exchange one cage for another? On the other hand, remaining a spinster was not appealing either — and she believed it would kill her mother if she were never to have the joy of seeing her only child married and having children of her own. And Kate loved children. Was there no way out?

★   ★   ★

Lady Follett's annual ball was well known as one of the highlights of the London season. This year, as always, she held it in her house in Hanover Square. It was a lovely June evening and the big salon on the first floor was filled with swags of early summer flowers.

A string quartet was playing Haydn's music in one corner of the room, while downstairs the silver dishes on the supper tables were filled with lobster salad, cold guinea fowl and quails' eggs.

Mrs Roscoe, splendid in midnight-blue satin and diamonds, was delighted to shake the hostess's gloved hand and introduce her daughter.

'Ah, Miss Kate Roscoe,' Lady Follett boomed, peering at Kate's small, slender figure and her bright red hair which had been simply arranged in a large chignon. 'Well, my dear, I hope you are going to have a delightful evening and perhaps make some new friends.' Her eyes moved onto the next guests in the reception line, one of whom was a European princess.

It was soon apparent, however, that there were plenty of others who had a great deal of interest in Miss Roscoe from the north, who was rumoured to be worth close on a million, and before long she had enough requests to fill almost all of her dance card.

Though Kate did not much care for the upper-class men she had met in London, it was impossible to be unhappy whilst wearing an elegant gown in pale green silk with little puffed sleeves and a train trimmed with cream guipure lace. Around her neck was a simple pearl necklace and in her hair, one cream silk rose. As Haydn's music played, she felt her heart take wing.

But two hours later, having had her toes trodden on by a number of clumsy dancing partners and her ears battered with talk of cricket and horse racing, she grew bored. Seeing her mother happily engaged in conversation with two other matrons, she slipped downstairs to find a bite to eat.

Lord Walton, one of her previous dance partners, spotted her as she stood considering the merits of the lobster against the salmon mayonnaise. In Kate's eyes, Lord Walton was a self-satisfied young man who seemed interested in very little except horse trading and having 'the odd flutter' at the tables, which she thought sounded ominous. Especially as his ancient family were well known to have fallen on hard times, and needed to preserve all the precious assets they still had.

'Why not try both, Miss Roscoe?' the young man urged. 'You're just like a little bird — you need some fattening up.' He chortled loudly at his jest.

She could tell that he had been enjoying a generous amount of Mrs Follett's fine wines. His face was very red and his steps somewhat unsteady as he moved closer to the table to make his own choice.

'A little bird in a gilded cage,' she murmured with a wry smile. 'At least I don't have to sing for my supper.'

Lord Walton caught the last remark, threw back his head and guffawed like a braying donkey. Slightly alarmed, Kate stepped swiftly backwards, and found herself colliding with the man just behind her. The wine goblet he was holding was knocked out of his hand, crashing to the marble floor and shattering into pieces. His white tie and starched shirt were liberally spattered with purple drops of fine burgundy

She flushed in mortification. 'Oh, I am so sorry.'

'Please don't think any more of it, madam.' The man's words were kind but his face was grim and unsmiling.

'No, no. It was my fault.'

He stared at her. 'A lady is never at fault,' he said, summoning a passing waiter to clear up the debris on the floor.

'Well, I think I am, in this particular case,' she countered, holding her ground and offering him a rueful smile. 'And I am truly sorry.' She bit her lip. 'I am afraid your shirt is ruined.'

'I have a very good valet who will take care of it,' he answered.

She stared up at him, both impressed and slightly intimidated by his tall, spare figure and his cleanly-cut but gaunt features. His hair was black, with a touch of silver at the temples. His eyes, a dark sapphire blue, were glinting and slightly narrowed as he made a steady evaluation of her face.

'There is no need to trouble yourself any further, madam,' he said. 'And perhaps you would excuse me now.' He gave her a slight bow, then turned and walked away towards the library.

Kate stood very still, finding herself somewhat unnerved by this short interchange. The grim-faced man's voice echoed in her head like a gentle reproof. Although she had to admit that it was a very pleasant, low-pitched voice, and without any of the affectations adopted by many of the London upper set who thought it smart to put on an artificial drawl, with a great deal of lisping and pronouncing their r's as if they were w's.

The guffawing Lord Walton had wandered away. Kate slipped through the wide French doors and walked out into the garden to eat her lobster and salmon in the calm of the evening. Eventually, knowing her mother would be fretting at her absence from the salon, she reluctantly went back upstairs. The thought of another two hours dancing with tipsy young men was not appealing. How lovely it would be to go home and sit reading in bed!

Mrs Roscoe was still in conversation

with one of the other ambitious mothers, but on seeing Kate, her smiling expression instantly switched to one of anxious disapproval. 'Kate, my dear, I have been constantly looking around trying to find you. Where have you been all this time?'

'I went to get some supper, Mama.'

Mrs Roscoe frowned. 'You should have waited for me, my dear.'

'I'm sorry. Would you like me to accompany you downstairs now? The buffet is very fine.'

Before her mother could answer, Lord Walton appeared, asking if he might place his name on Kate's card for a further dance. Kate felt a spark of panic. Walton was clearly drunk now, and the thought of dancing with him was positively repulsive. She felt her mother shift in her chair, torn between wanting her to encourage the young man, at the same time disapproving of his inebriated state.

'I seem to have mislaid my card,' Kate said smoothly, thinking that an evasion of the truth was justified in the circumstances.

'Hmm. Well, when you find it, Miss Roscoe, perhaps you would put my name on it. Or perhaps you prefer the company of the Earl of Gresham,' Walton said, his voice sulky and sarcastic beneath his slurred, lisping tone.

Kate's spine stiffened. 'I'm sorry, Lord Walton, I don't believe I know anyone of that name.'

'No? Then it's strange that you seemed to be deep in conversation with him at the supper table.'

Kate recalled the hawk-faced man whose shirt she had ruined through her clumsiness. She stared up at the young aristocrat, lost for words.

'You should be careful around Gresham,' Lord Walton muttered. 'He has quite a reputation.' He bowed solemnly to her and to her mother. 'Good evening, ladies,' he said, moving away with comically staggering steps.

Mrs Roscoe's eyes were huge with conjecture. 'I think we need to retire to the ladies' rest room,' she decided, rising to her feet. 'Come along, Kate.'

Kate had the sense her mother would drag her by force if she offered any challenge, so she duly followed her parent as she marched from the salon.

The ladies' rest room was momentarily quiet, apart from an attendant dusting around the basins and water jugs. Mrs Roscoe gave a brief nod in the woman's direction and then drew Kate into a far corner of the room.

'Who is this Earl of Gresham?'

'I have no idea, Mama.'

'And yet you were in conversation with him.'

'Unfortunately I bumped into him and made him drop his wine glass.'

Mrs Roscoe raised a hand to stop her at that point. 'Kate! You haven't been drinking wine have you?'

'No, Mama. I was standing near the supper table and I stepped backwards rather sharply to avoid the attentions of Lord Walton.'

'And then stepped on this Earl of

Gresham's toe?'

'Yes. And obviously I stopped to make apologies.'

A war between relief and disappointment was going on in Mrs Roscoe's racing thoughts. 'And what is he like?'

'Tall, dark, rather stern-looking. And he wasn't wearing a coronet,' Kate finished mischievously.

'Silly girl. Concentrate on what's important. Is he young? Is he married?'

'Mama, I'm sorry, I have no idea.' Kate was fairly sure, however, that her mother would be in possession of the relevant information about the Earl's person and circumstances before much time had passed.

'Very well,' Mrs Roscoe said, drawing a line under this brief interchange. 'We shall go back into the salon now, and if you see the Earl, please be good enough to point him out to me. Did you introduce yourself?' she added, as an afterthought.

'No,' Kate replied. 'And neither did he.'

Her mama gave a heavy sigh. 'Come along!' she said.

Back in the salon, they were surprised to note that a small drama was taking place. It appeared that one of the violinists in the quartet ensemble had had to retire feeling unwell, and the other players were wondering whether they felt able to carry on without him. Lady Follett, who had been conferring with the group, now stepped forward and clapped her hands to gain attention.

'My Lords, ladies and gentlemen,' she said. 'Unfortunately our lead violinist is temporarily indisposed. If there is any gentleman present who could take his place, I would be most grateful for their services.'

There was a long hush.

Kate felt a spark of excitement shoot up inside her. She knew she could easily step into the breach. But it was not considered ladylike to put oneself forward, and as her mother often reminded her when she practised on her violin, a lady should confine herself to the piano and singing as regarded musical accomplishments. Her sense of frustration at being here at this ball, like a prize brood mare up for the highest bidder because of her money, suddenly hit her in all its humiliating crudeness.

She had already stepped forward and begun speaking before her mind had consciously planned it. 'I am happy to offer my musical services, Lady Follett,' she said in her clear sweet voice.

Lady Follett raised her lorgnette and regarded Kate with a degree of not altogether pleasant surprise. Quickly recovering herself, she said, 'Miss Roscoe. How kind. Please do step up onto the dais.'

The three male players looked doubtfully at Kate as she sat in the absent violinist's seat and proceeded to tune his instrument.

'We were thinking of playing music from Mozart's German Dances for the next two dances,' the cellist whispered to her, looking a trifle anxious.

Kate looked at the music on the stand. She was a good sight reader of music, but it helped that she also knew these particular pieces and felt confident to play them. She glanced around the other players. 'Shall we give it a try? I shall do my best.'

The second violin player took the lead and counted them in with nods of his head. As the music flowed from her bow, Kate forgot about the gilded, garlanded salon, about the self-satisfied, dull young men she had been obliged to dance with, about her mother's reaction to seeing her daughter playing on the stage with a group of hired musicians. As she worked with them to create this beautiful sound from the pen of a composer who had such wit and charm, all other sensation was temporarily shut out. Dimly she was aware of the dancers gliding around the floor, and the nods of encouragement and approval from her fellow players.

Fresh music was placed on the stand and there was more playing. Energy flowed through her, streaking her face with moisture, dampening her hair so that the tendrils around her face began to curl. And all too soon, it was all over. They played the National Anthem, then stood to acknowledge the applause of the assembled guests. As Kate's musician companions gathered around to shake her hand, and push her gently forward on the dais, the applause became wildly enthusiastic. There were hurrahs, and bravos and even a few whistles.

Kate curtsied and smiled. At the corner of her vision she was suddenly aware of the dark, granite-faced Earl of Gresham. Except that now his lips were curved into a faint smile as he applauded. For a second, their glances met and Kate felt an unnerving jolt of electricity chase down her spine. But as she stepped down from the dais, walking through the smiling assembly in search of her mother, she noticed that he had completely vanished.

2

Kate woke to a gentle tapping on her bedroom door and called out, 'Come in.' She pulled herself into a sitting position as her maid, Beatrice, known as Bea, came in with a breakfast tray.

'Good morning, miss,' Bea said, placing the tray on the bedside table and then drawing the curtains.

'What is this, Bea?' Kate asked, eyeing the tea, toast and marmalade. 'I was planning to get up for breakfast as usual.'

'I thought you might like to have a few minutes to yourself, Miss,' Bea said, her eyes full of meaning.

Kate shot her a glance. 'Let me guess,' she said. 'My mama is not pleased with me.'

'She is not in a good mood, Miss,' Bea said diplomatically.

Kate sighed. 'Oh dear.'

'She told me to say that she expects to see you in the drawing room at ten o'clock sharp.'

That sounded ominous, Kate thought, taking a nibble of toast.

Bea gave a little cough.

'Now what is it?' Kate asked, smiling.

'You said I could have the morning and afternoon off, Miss. It's my sister's birthday. Will that still be suitable for you?'

'Yes, of course, Bea.'

'Thank you, Miss. Shall I get out your blue silk?'

Kate shrugged. 'Whatever you think is best for the weather today. And you needn't bother to dress my hair, I'll do it myself. You get ready and go off to see your sister.'

Bea beamed. 'You're very kind, Miss Roscoe.'

'I hope you a lovely time today,' Kate said, as Bea stood in the doorway.

'And you too, Miss.' Bea gave the slightest lift of her eyebrows. *Rather you than me,* she seemed to be saying, mindful of Kate's meeting with her mother later on.

Kate finished her toast, washed quickly and got dressed. As she brushed her hair and arranged it in a roll at the nape of her neck, she anticipated her mother's protests and tried to assemble some points of defence.

As it turned out, Mrs Roscoe had decided to make a huge effort to be reasonable in her remarks to her daughter. At first.

'Let's sit down together and have a talk, dear,' she said, standing rigidly beside the fireplace as Kate entered the drawing room.

Kate could see that her mother had been pacing up and down; there were little tell-tale tracks in the thick Persian rug.

Kate duly seated herself. Her mother remained standing.

'Kate, I know you do not share my views on some issues,' her mother began. 'However, I do feel that I have to draw your attention to some aspects of your behaviour yesterday evening, in the hope that we can come to some agreement of how you might choose to — how can I put it? — alter your behaviour in the future.'

Kate felt a flame of rebellion flicker within. 'Is this connected with my volunteering to play in the quartet?' she asked, her tone uncompromising.

'Well — partly, my dear.' Mrs Roscoe paused.

'What then, Mama?'

'It is your whole attitude, Kate. Your flippancy regarding the serious issue of finding a husband worries me a good deal. You must realise that a young woman in your position, in possession of a very handsome dowry, needs a husband to offer her social standing — and, of course, a steadying and guiding hand as regards the money.'

'When I marry, most of my money will be passed over to my husband,' Kate pointed out. 'He will be able to do as he likes with it.'

'That is only right and proper. Men

understand about these matters.'

'Do they, Mama? Do you think a brainless young man such as Lord Walton would understand about such matters?'

'I am sure he is not brainless. And he would have excellent advisors.'

'I could have excellent advisors,' Kate countered, wondering how long she could maintain her self-control. 'In fact, I could afford the very best advisors, could I not?'

Mrs Roscoe let out a gasp of irritation. 'It is a man's place to deal with financial matters. It is a woman's place to marry, to be a good, obedient wife and bear children. Everyone sees the sense in that. So should you.'

'Well I do not,' Kate said quietly.

'You stupid girl!' her mother burst out, all efforts at reasonableness suddenly thrown to the winds. 'You shamed me last night. You drew attention to yourself in the worst possible manner. First of all you presumed to be cool and offhand with an eligible member of the aristocracy, and then you clumsily trod on another aristocrat's foot. And to crown it all, you pushed yourself forward to join with a band of paid musicians.'

She stopped, breathing heavily, overcome with her sense of the injustice at having produced such a wayward daughter.

'There is nothing dishonourable about playing music in public, Mama,' Kate said with dangerous quietness. 'And certain members of the company listening seemed to appreciate my efforts.'

'Hah! Much in the way they appreciate the prancing of vulgar chorus girls. For goodness' sake, some of the gentlemen even went as far as to *whistle*.' Mrs Roscoe sagged slightly against the mantelpiece.

Usually, at this point in Kate's disputes with her mother she was inclined to back down, knowing that however disagreeable her mother's protests might be, they were honest and deeply felt. But this morning she was so annoyed at her mother's comments that she felt the need to fight her corner.

'Mama,' she said, warning herself to keep her voice low and calm. 'I am indeed sorry if I upset you, but in my own view I did nothing terribly wrong.'

'Good heavens, Kate! Are you completely insensitive regarding what are considered good behaviour and manners in society? How dared you presume to be so offhand with Lord Walton? He was obviously interested in you. You should at least have been civil to him.'

'He is an idle fool, who likes wine and gambling. Last night, Mama, he was a drunken idle fool. Is he the kind of husband you would wish for me?'

Mrs Roscoe was torn. 'I admit he must have drunk a little more wine than was good for him. But then young men must be permitted a few high jinks. He will be a duke one day, Kate. And you could be a duchess.'

Kate jumped up, fury racing through

her veins like a shot of brandy. 'I can see that we are not going to reach an agreement on the issue of last night,' she said. 'If you would excuse me, I think I shall go for a short walk.'

'Wait!' her mother commanded. 'What about the Earl of Gresham?'

Kate had almost reached the door. 'What of him, Mama?'

'I gather he is a widower, most likely seeking a wife. And I was also told that he was extremely attentive to your violin playing.'

Kate turned, hardly able to believe her ears at the ways her mother could twist situations to suit her own purposes. 'Well, at least that should be a comfort for me,' she said, sweeping through the door and shutting it firmly.

'Come here, Kate!' she heard her mother call. But Kate ran swiftly up the stairs to her own room, panting with frustration as she shut the door.

She splashed cold water on her face and paced to and fro, her feelings agitated and confused. She knew she must leave the house and its repressive atmosphere for a while. A walk would surely be calming.

Recalling that her maid Bea had the day off and therefore could not accompany her, she hesitated. Walking out alone through the London streets was not considered the done thing for well-bred young ladies. She bit on her lip. Surely it would do no harm just to take the air, walk in the park for a time — maybe venture up in the direction of the Exeter Hall, where she and Bea had attended meetings on a couple of occasions.

She changed into her fawn walking dress and a hat with a pull-down veil, then crept down the stairs, tip-toed past the drawing room and slid through the front door, closing it with the softest click.

It was a pleasant morning, the sky a vivid blue, dotted with puffy white clouds. Kate breathed in the soft air and instantly felt better. Her mind was so full of the recent bitter altercation with her mother that as she walked on, she was only half conscious of where she was heading. Eventually, without really meaning to, she found herself approaching the Exeter Hall. The posters outside advertised a public lecture to be given by Mrs G. J. Winchester, entitled *The Role of Women: The Way Forward.*

Kate had been to two similar meetings with related themes. She had found the speakers' ideas both disturbing and stimulating, although Bea thought they were a lot of poppycock. But this one sounded too good to miss — and it was due to start in less than five minutes.

Kate drew some deep breaths and walked through the doors into the imposing auditorium. The audience was quite small, maybe a hundred at most. She sat quietly on a seat towards the back of the hall. A pleasant-faced young man sat at the other end of the row, and as she glanced towards him he smiled and dipped his head in polite acknowledgement of her presence.

Mrs Winchester was a fiery speaker,

urging her audience to deplore the current treatment of women, regarded as mere chattels to be ordered about by men — indeed, as if they were little more than dumb animals. Kate could see an element of truth in that, although she knew a number of women, her mother included, who seemed perfectly able to rule the house and their husbands as well. Mrs Winchester went on to explain that women had just as much sense, judgement and personal integrity as men which was well demonstrated in the domestic scene — yet still, in the eyes of the law, they had very little status. The words sank into Kate's thoughts, ideas she would examine in the quietness of her own room later.

At the end of the lecture she walked out into the West End, planning to hail a cab to take her home. Clouds had gathered, and Piccadilly was packed with people hurrying to finish their shopping as rain began to fall. On several occasions, young men seeing a well-dressed lady walking on her own tipped their hats roguishly, and there were a few winks and even suggestive remarks. She hurried on, becoming increasingly uneasy.

Suddenly a loaded rag and bone cart swerved as the horse drawing it slipped on the damp cobbles. Kate heard a crash as the cart overturned and a piece of old iron piping flew at her, catching her on the side of her face and causing her fall to heavily onto the stones. Stunned, she tried to sit up.

She heard a voice address her softly. 'Do please permit me to help.' An arm reached out to steady her as she struggled shakily to her feet. Her head ached, and when she put her hand up to her cheekbone, she felt the sticky warmth of blood.

Her young rescuer put his arm firmly around her and half carried her to a doorway. Unlocking the door, he led her inside and settled her onto a rather shabby sofa in a little parlour filled with piles of books and papers.

'Take some deep breaths,' he suggested.

Kate took his advice, and slowly began to recover herself. Looking up, she saw that he was the same young man who had been seated on her row at the lecture. He smiled at her reassuringly, then disappeared, quickly returning with an older woman who brought with her a basin of warm water, some clean rags and a bandage.

'My landlady, Mrs James,' he explained.

Whilst sympathetic to Kate's plight, and ministering to her very gently, Mrs James set about scolding the young man for bringing a lady into the house. But when she realised that Kate seemed a very respectable young lady, she softened. 'What were you doing, walking about the streets on your own, Miss?' she asked. 'What will your poor mother think?'

What indeed, Kate thought, her heart sinking. When Mrs James had completed her ministrations, Kate rose stiffly to her feet, wishing to return home, knowing that her mother would be worried about her. Oh, what a fool she had been, flouncing thoughtlessly from the house.

'You must not go alone,' the young man said. 'I shall escort you to a cab and see that you are safely on your way.'

Kate thanked him and, as she still felt unsteady, she was glad to take his arm when he offered it. As they walked into the street, a party of young men were passing, talking and jesting loudly. Kate saw that one of them was the effete Lord Walton. Instinctively she drew her arm away from the protection of her rescuer, but she knew Walton had already seen her. *Could things get any worse?* she wondered.

On reaching home, she had no need to let herself in with her key. Her mother was at the window looking up and down the square, and she hurried into the entrance hall to open the door herself.

On seeing Kate's bruised face, Mrs Roscoe's stern expression was replaced with one of horror.

'I had a fall on the cobbles, Mama,'

Kate said, trying to reassure her. 'A rag and bone cart turned over and I was in the way!' She gave a rueful smile, grimacing as the muscles of her face protested at being required to move. 'It is only bruising,' she added hastily. 'No bones broken.'

'I have been utterly beside myself with alarm,' Mrs Roscoe told her, pulling Kate into the drawing room and pushing her, none too gently, into a chair. 'Oh — your poor face is in a dreadful state. We shall have to cancel our engagements until you are fully recovered.' She shook her head. 'I'll ring for the housekeeper to bring a cold compress to relieve the swelling.'

'Thank you, Mama,' Kate said. 'I am sorry to have caused you distress.'

'But where have you been, all this time? And surely you realise how improper it is to walk out on your own!'

'I walked through the park,' Kate told her, 'and then on to the West End.' Well, at least that was the truth — if not the whole story.

'I do hope you did not see any of our friends,' Mrs Roscoe fretted. 'What would they have thought seeing you on your own? They would think I am a most neglectful mother. It really is too bad of you to be so wayward.'

'I saw none of our friends,' Kate said, miserable to be telling half-truths and white lies. But the whole truth would only upset her mother afresh.

The housekeeper hurried in with the cold compress and Mrs Roscoe was obliged to cease her scolding. And by the time she and Kate went in to dinner, they were on cordial terms once more.

★　★　★

When Kate looked into her mirror the next morning, she was alarmed to see that her bruises had become even more colourful than before. A broad sweep of purple ran down the edge of her cheek like a storm cloud. Around the lower part of her eye was a deep scarlet half-circle of blood lying beneath the skin, as finely drawn as though an artist had painted it.

'If I go out like this I shall frighten the horses,' she teased her reflection.

When Bea came in with a tray of toast and hot chocolate, she let out a little yelp of dismay. 'Miss Roscoe! How did it come about that you got a face like that?'

Kate repeated the story she had told to her mother.

Bea listened carefully, giving little clucks of sympathy. But Kate saw the conjecture in her eyes, the concern that Kate had flouted convention by walking out on her own.

'Did you have a pleasant day with your sister?' Kate asked, not prepared to go into any further details.

Bea chatted happily about her day off, at the same time experimenting with ways to dress Kate's hair so as to conceal the bruising.

'There,' she said. 'I've got your cheek covered nicely, but I don't know what we can do about your poor eye.'

'Well, if I go out I shall have to wear a heavy veil,' Kate said cheerfully.

'And make sure you have a companion,' Bea said firmly. 'If you'll excuse my being so bold, Miss.'

As it turned out the day was fine and warm, and Mrs Roscoe was in favour of taking a little turn in the park herself. She had put on weight recently and her doctor had advised regular, gentle exercise.

'He told me that our dear Queen walks out every day, even when it is raining,' Mrs Roscoe told Kate, as she had mentioned many times before. 'But fortunately it is sunny today.'

'I'd like to come with you, Mama,' Kate said, hating to be penned up in the house. 'Perhaps we could take some bread to feed the ducks.'

Mrs Roscoe looked doubtful. 'Very well, my dear. At least I shall be able to keep my eye on you if we are together. It you put on a wide-brimmed hat and a pretty veil, I think you will do quite nicely. You could take a parasol for extra protection. I do not expect any of our friends will be out so early. And if we do see any of them, I shall simply say that you slipped on the outside steps yesterday when it was wet.'

So that is to be our story, thought Kate, giving a secret, wry smile.

The park was mainly peopled with nannies pushing babies in prams. At the edge of the lake, the ducks were swimming in circles quacking noisily at the prospect of food. Two small girls were watching them, under the careful supervision of their nursemaid.

Leaving her mother to take a short rest on a park bench, Kate went to stand close to the children, who both looked up and smiled at her.

'Hello,' said Kate, who was fond of children.

They both smiled back and then looked away, too shy to answer.

Kate opened her paper bag which the cook had kindly filled with sweet fairy cakes that were two days old and no longer suitable for serving to visitors. Some were plain, some chocolate and some coffee-flavoured. As she began to crumble them, the children watched her longingly. Kate was unsure whether they wanted something to feed to the ducks, or whether they had a fancy for eating the little cakes themselves.

She smiled at the nursemaid. 'Is it permitted for me to let the children feed some of these cakes to the ducks?'

The nursemaid was doubtful. 'I'm not sure their father would be happy.'

'I think their father would be perfectly happy about that,' a low voice responded. A voice Kate recognised instantly. A sharp shiver went down her spine. She bent down to the children and gave them a fairy cake each.

The Earl of Gresham came to stand beside her. He was very formal in a dark coat and narrow fawn trousers. 'Miss Roscoe,' he said. 'We meet again. Allow me to introduce myself.'

As he started on his courteous and highly correct introduction, Mrs Roscoe came hurrying forward.

'And this must be your mama,' the Earl remarked, giving Mrs Roscoe a faint smile which seemed to throw her into an uncharacteristic fluster. 'The Earl of Gresham, at your service, madam.'

'Earl Gresham,' Mrs Roscoe answered politely, recovering herself. 'I believe my daughter has met you previously.'

'Indeed. She stepped on my foot and caused me to spill my wine.'

'Yes, she was so sorry for that,' Mrs Roscoe said hastily. 'As was I.'

The Earl turned to Kate. She sensed that the ironic smile he gave her was verging on the conspiratorial, as though they were sharing a private joke.

'May I congratulate you, Miss Roscoe, on your very accomplished and sensitive playing in Mrs Follett's salon,' he said.

'Thank you, sir,' Kate responded, looking up at him through her veil, thinking how very attractive he was when he smiled, and hugging his words of praise to herself.

'Of course, Kate does not usually play in public,' Mrs Roscoe explained.

The Earl nodded. 'Does your daughter study with a famous maestro of the violin?' he enquired, fixing Mrs Roscoe with his unswerving gaze.

'Er, no,' Mrs Roscoe confessed. 'Her former governess taught her to read music and familiarised her with the violin.'

'I am surprised,' said the Earl. 'A talent such as your daughter's should surely merit the tuition of a virtuoso. I would be happy to recommend her to my friend, Mr Igor Voronsky, who — as you will know — is renowned throughout the world in music circles.'

'That is most kind of you, sir,' said Mrs Roscoe, who knew nothing of a man with such a name as Voronsky, musician or otherwise.

'Do you mean that?' Kate broke in, forgetting all etiquette regarding the way to address an earl and staring up at him in excited disbelief.

'Indeed, I do, Miss Roscoe.'

She received the impression that he did not make promises lightly.

'Then, thank you,' she said, though she was not sure she wished to be under the tutelage of a great virtuoso. She simply loved playing her violin.

The little girls had come back to her for more fairy cakes, tugging at her skirt and looking up at her with winning smiles. She turned to the Earl.

'May I give them some more?'

'You may,' he said gravely.

'They are lovely children,' she observed warmly.

'Yes,' he agreed. 'But they are sad children, too. They have no mother. My wife died shortly after giving birth to them.'

Kate stared up at him, seeing his face bleak with loss. 'Oh, I am so very sorry!' she exclaimed, a wave of genuine sympathy flowing from her.

'So am I,' he said, softly. 'And now, I am afraid I must take my leave. We are due to call on the children's aunt. She is very firm on the issue of punctuality. Good day, Mrs Roscoe and Miss Roscoe.' He nodded courteously to them and lifted the children into their perambulator. The nursemaid grasped the handle and the little party moved off.

'Well!' exclaimed Mrs Roscoe, her face alight with excitement, her ability to make any kind of verbal comment having temporarily deserted her. 'I think I need to sit down for a few moments.' She retreated to the park bench and dabbed her face with a lace handkerchief.

In the drawing room after lunch, Kate was subjected to her mother's nonstop conjecture. 'The Earl is a fine and handsome gentleman,' she mused. 'I am told he has three houses, huge estates and an immense fortune.'

'And two lovely children,' Kate added, noting that her mama had clearly not spent the entirety of the previous day consumed with anxiety about her daughter's whereabouts, but had also taken the opportunity to find out as much as possible regarding the Earl of Gresham from her afternoon callers.

'Yes, indeed, the children!' Mrs Roscoe cocked her head and regarded her daughter. 'And the Earl made a point of telling you that those poor children had no mother. In fact, do you know, it almost seemed to me that he was thinking you might be just the lady to take on the role of mama to those dear little children.'

Kate laughed off her mother's fantasies. But the images of the little scene in the park kept playing inside her head, and through the night the compelling aristocrat featured in her dreams, driving out all the humiliation of the Piccadilly incident. She had to admit that the Earl of Gresham's person and demeanour were magnetically appealing to her, and that his children were delightful. Not only that, but the Earl seemed to share her love of music and playing — and she knew that he had not been jesting when he spoke of finding her a prestigious tutor.

*   *   *

At breakfast, she touched her face, feeling tentatively around the bruises. Surely the Earl of Gresham had noticed them — but as a perfect gentleman, he had given no indication. She gave a little sigh.

'Are you quite well, Kate?' her mother enquired.

'Yes, mama. Just a little tired.'

'After all that to-do yesterday I am not surprised,' her mother said. 'Go and lie down, my dear, and recover yourself before any callers arrive.'

Kate went upstairs to her bedroom and stood at the window. Could it be that she was feeling what Jane Eyre had felt for Mr Rochester when she took up residence in Thornfield Hall? Had she, Kate Roscoe, finally fallen in love?

In the drawing room, Mrs Roscoe permitted herself the secret pleasure of planning a very grand wedding. For weeks now she had despaired of Kate's ever agreeing to marry anyone. She had been like the proverbial horse one could take to water but not compel to drink. But her mother's instinct told her that Kate was by no means indifferent to the Earl of Gresham — and he, for his part, seemed exceedingly taken with her.

There was a deferential knock on the door and her butler, Grantley, came in bearing a letter on a silver plate. 'Thank you, Grantley.' Mrs Roscoe looked at the letter in astonishment; it was of thick beige vellum, sealed with a fat red seal bearing the coat of arms of Lord Walton.

Good heavens, she thought, her heart fluttering. *What now? Is my little girl about to have another suitor?* She reached for the paper knife. The writing inside was bold and flowery.

Dear Mrs Roscoe,
I write to you on behalf of my brother, Lord Walton, on a matter of the utmost delicacy.

47

My brother has mentioned to me that when he was walking with friends in town yesterday, he happened to see your daughter, Miss Kate Roscoe, leaving a gentleman's lodgings in Piccadilly, her arm linked with his. Miss Roscoe was without a chaperone. Pray be assured that neither my brother nor I believe that there was any serious harm in this, but we felt you should be apprised of the incident, and that Miss Roscoe should be advised that it would be most unsuitable for such an outing to be repeated.

Naturally, my brother and I will say nothing further regarding this matter. However we cannot entirely vouch for the silence of each and every one of my brother's acquaintances who were also witnesses to the event.

I am very sorry to give you this distressing news, dear madam, but I can assure you it is sent in both your own and Miss Roscoe's best interests.

With the most sincere regards,
Lady Gwendolyn Walton.

Mrs Roscoe stared at the letter, the words seeming to spin before her eyes. The blood drained from her face. She was shrewd enough to read between the lines. Lady Gwendolyn was suggesting that Kate had been conducting an illicit affair with some low young man. Moreover she was hinting that news of this matter could quite easily become public knowledge.

She did not believe that Kate could be involved in an illicit relationship. But what had really been going on in Piccadilly the day before? She felt panic rising at the possibility of society's doors closing on her, of people being 'Not at Home' when she called. This could be a scandal from which Kate — and she herself — might never recover.

She rang for Grantley. 'Tell Miss Kate that I wish to speak with her,' she announced. 'Immediately.'

Grantley went on his stately way. 'Immediately' had little meaning for him where anxious ladies were concerned. As he closed the door of the drawing room, the doorbell rang. He hesitated for a second, then went to open it. A tall, hawk-faced gentleman, whom he recognised, and a similarly raptor-faced lady stood on the doorstep.

'The Earl of Gresham and Lady Helen Spence requesting to know if Mrs Roscoe is At Home,' the Earl said with quiet, yet steely, authority.

Grantley sensed excitement in the offing. He bowed and went to speak with Mrs Roscoe.

'What? Who?' she cried, springing up from her chair. Her thoughts skittered for a few seconds. 'Show them in, please. And then bring some tea, cucumber sandwiches and muffins.'

'Very well, madam. Shall I request Miss Roscoe to join you, as you requested earlier?' he asked silkily.

Mrs Roscoe swallowed. 'Not for the present.'

Lady Helen entered the room first. She was dressed in a ruby-red Balmoral mantle and her bonnet was decorated with nodding ostrich plumes. The Earl of Gresham followed, smoothly greeting Mrs Roscoe and introducing his sister.

Lady Helen sat down, drawing off her gloves. The Earl sat opposite her, crossing his long legs. His face was stern and solemn. 'Mrs Roscoe, I have come to speak with you on a sensitive matter concerning Miss Roscoe.'

Mrs Roscoe's heart began to thump.

'I was wondering if Miss Roscoe was at home,' he continued.

'Yes, indeed.'

'Then perhaps she would care to join us. I do not wish to speak of her in her absence. That would seem unfair.'

Mrs Roscoe's mouth fell open. She had never met anyone quite so direct, quite so daunting. She rang for Grantley, who arrived with the tea and sandwiches.

'Will you inform Miss Roscoe that our visitors would like to see her,' she told Grantley, confident that he would present Kate with a short and accurate picture of the situation.

Sure enough, before Mrs Roscoe had finished pouring the tea, Kate entered the room, her bruised face pale and full of conjecture.

The Earl rose to his feet. 'Miss Roscoe,' he said, taking her hand as she held it out and holding it for a fraction of a second longer than necessary.

Kate gazed up at him, the sense of joy in seeing him again crowding out all other sensations. He then introduced Lady Helen. They all sat down again and the Earl accepted a cup of tea and a cucumber sandwich.

He turned to Kate. 'Miss Roscoe, I believe that there was an unfortunate incident yesterday when you fell on the pavement owing to some altercation with a rag and bone cart.'

'Yes, indeed,' Kate agreed. *How do you know that?* she wondered.

'It was an unfortunate accident,' Mrs Roscoe broke in, to trying to stave off what might be coming next.

'I trust your injuries are not too serious,' the Earl said to Kate, who touched her bruised cheek and gave a rueful smile.

'Some bruising, but thankfully nothing

more,' Mrs Roscoe rejoined.

'I am glad to hear it.' The Earl paused. 'What I was not glad to hear was that Miss Roscoe was seen in the company of a young gentleman yesterday, leaving his lodgings in Piccadilly.'

Despite herself Kate felt the blood rush to her face in a flood of warmth.

Mrs Roscoe sat up very straight, determined to muster the best response she could think of. 'Oh, dear. I assure you, Earl Gresham, that there is some simple explanation. My daughter is of excellent breeding and character, although she can be a little headstrong at times.'

Lady Helen gave a polite little cough. Kate suddenly felt as though she were the accused in the witness box at the Old Bailey.

'I agree with you,' the Earl said to Mrs Roscoe. 'I am sure Miss Roscoe would never do anything to bring shame on herself or you, madam. Moreover the information I have received is from a source I do not consider entirely reliable.'

He is on my side, thought Kate, amazed and bewildered. She was emboldened to speak up for herself, wishing the Earl to know the full truth of what had happened in Piccadilly. And it was also only fair to her mother to speak out. She addressed her three listeners in a clear, steady voice.

'Yesterday morning I wished to go for a walk. My maid was engaged with her family and I rashly made the decision to go alone. I walked as far as Piccadilly and I saw that there was a lecture about to begin the Exeter Hall. It was on women's rights.' She saw her mother's look of dismay, but continued nevertheless. 'I went in and sat at the back. A young man was sitting close by and he made a polite acknowledgement of my presence. When I left the hall, as I walked along hoping to hail a cab, I was hit by an object from an overturned rag and bone cart.' She indicated her bruises.

'I fell and was temporarily stunned. The young man I had met at the Exeter Hall was just behind me. He helped me up and took me to his lodgings, where his landlady kindly attended to my injuries. And after that he escorted me to a cab. I admit that I was leaning on his arm, as I still felt somewhat unsteady. And then I returned home.' She finished, glancing at her mother, then folding her hands in her lap and staring down at them.

There was a silence in the room.

'You are most eloquent, Miss Roscoe,' the Earl told her. 'And most convincing.' He considered for a few moments. 'Nevertheless,' he continued, 'I know that the source is something of a mischief-maker and I fear could make considerable trouble for Miss Roscoe if he chose to do so.'

'Yes,' Mrs Roscoe whispered.

Kate was desperately trying to work out what was going on. She could only assume Lord Walton or one of his friends was putting about the news of what they had seen in Piccadilly the day before. Her heart sank. Despite what she had said, the Earl had every reason to believe that she was either a shameless flirt or a very foolish girl. And yet she could still feel his sympathy flowing out towards her.

'Our London society is very unforgiving,' the Earl said gravely. 'Rumours about young ladies can cause a great deal of trouble, humiliation and suffering. The lady and her family might find themselves cruelly ostracised.'

Remorse coursed through Kate's body. She glanced at Lady Helen, wondering what she was thinking of all this. The lady's face was blank.

'I am here to offer a possible solution to the problem,' the Earl said calmly. 'I have come with an offer for Miss Roscoe's hand in marriage. If Miss Roscoe becomes the Countess of Gresham, I should think that would be sufficient to quell any rumours. And if not, you may be sure that I know exactly how to deal with the perpetrator.'

Kate stared at him, astounded. Mrs Roscoe swayed in her chair and was not revived until smelling salts were administered.

3

Have you entirely taken leave of your senses, Rupert?' Lady Helen asked as they both settled themselves in the Earl's carriage, having taken their farewells of Mrs and Miss Roscoe.

Her brother, as usual, merely raised his eyebrows and said nothing, which Lady Helen found most annoying.

'You know nothing of this girl. You have spent only minutes in her presence. I am aware that you are a man who is fearless in making decisions, but this offer of marriage seems somewhat extreme.'

'Indeed, I have made it my business to find out quite as much as I need about the young lady. She comes from a highly respected family from Northumberland. Neither Miss Roscoe, nor her mother or her late father have ever been under any shadow of scandal. She is most likely not fully conversant with the ways of London society, but she is obviously a young woman of intelligence and integrity.'

'How do you know she is not a cunning little fortune hunter?'

'Because she has a fortune of around a million pounds.'

Lady Helen's elegant head gave a little jerk. 'Really. That does rather add to her charms.'

'Moreover, my children could talk of nothing but the nice lady in the park until they went to bed last night.'

'Indeed.'

'And Miss Roscoe plays the violin like an angel.'

Lady Helen briefly closed her eyes. 'Some men fall for a pair of delightful blue eyes — but you, my dear brother, seem to be enchanted with ladies who can weave magic spells with music.'

'Josefa was a brilliant pianist,' the Earl murmured sadly.

Lady Helen sighed. 'Your dear late wife was a wild Hungarian princess,' she said. 'And altogether rather special.'

'Yes,' the Earl agreed.

'Do you think it is fair to ask this young country girl from the North to follow in her footsteps?'

'I do not expect that of her.'

'So pray tell me — what exactly, then, it is that you do expect of her?'

The Earl was silent for some moments. 'Companionship,' he said in his low, chocolaty voice. He seemed about to elaborate further and then stopped himself.

'A mother for your children?' Lady Helen enquired.

'Yes, indeed. That is most important.'

Lady Helen leaned back against the velvet upholstery. 'Well, there is no point in my remonstrating with you,' she said. 'You always do exactly as you please.'

He gave a small smile.

'But then, you are a peer of the realm,' she went on. 'And very rich. I suppose it is not surprising that you please yourself.'

When they reached Grosvenor Square,

the Earl jumped out to hand his sister down. She reached up and kissed his cheek. 'What about Mrs Cheveney?' she asked, raising her eyebrows.

'Ah, yes,' he said, his face still and thoughtful. 'Mrs Cheveney.'

★ ★ ★

Mrs Roscoe came down for dinner dressed as she imagined was fitting for the forthcoming mother-in-law of an earl. Her gown was of gold shot silk with pagoda sleeves, her hair formed into a massive chignon complete with twirls of false ringlets. The diamonds around her neck flashed fire with each breath. And her breaths were coming deep and fast.

Her talk was firstly of the Earl's main residence, Gresham Abbey in Derbyshire. Of how Kate might wish to refurbish the main rooms, which was a bride's prerogative. How she would give grand balls at the Earl's London mansion close by Kensington Palace.

'The Earl has not formally asked me to marry him,' pointed out Kate, not able to get a word in until they reached the pudding — a delicious lemon posset laced with a touch of Fino sherry.

'Of course he will ask you. He made his intentions clear before both myself and his sister.'

'And what do you think I should answer?' Kate asked mischievously.

Her mother's brows snapped together. 'Good heavens! Don't tell me you are thinking of refusing, Kate. This is no time for your silly ideas. There is not a girl in the world who would not be prostrate with delight at being asked to marry the Earl of Gresham. He is a man of supreme breeding and, from what I hear, incredibly well-connected and rich.' She shook a warning her finger at her daughter. 'Don't you dare to go against all common sense — or indeed my wishes — as regards this matter.'

'No, I won't,' said Kate, putting a dainty spoonful of lemon possett into her mouth.

Her mother's spoon dropped onto the plate with a clatter. 'You won't marry him?' she croaked.

'No, I won't go against your wishes, Mama,' Kate said demurely, thinking how ironic it was that she found herself madly in love with exactly the sort of man her mother had hardly dared hope for in her wildest dreams.

'Well, that is some comfort,' sighed her mother. 'Oh dear, now I feel worried that maybe he won't ask after all. Maybe he will change his mind.'

'Oh, Mama!' Kate chided.

At that point, Grantley came in bearing another letter. This time the seal bore the coat of arms of the Earl of Gresham. Mrs Roscoe tore it open with shaking fingers. '*The Earl of Gresham will call tomorrow at four o'clock to see Mrs Roscoe and Miss Roscoe in order to make a proposal of marriage,*' she read out in triumph.

Kate's heart soared on wings. 'I wonder which one of us he is he going to propose to?' she joked, as she read through the note.

Mrs Roscoe glared at her. 'This is no time for jests, Kate. You will wear your aquamarine silk and I shall loan you my diamonds. You will accept the Earl's offer and that is that!'

★   ★   ★

At four o'clock precisely the next day, the Earl of Gresham presented himself in Mrs Roscoe's sitting room. Kate was standing beside the fireplace, numb with speculation and nervousness. Around her neck her mother's diamonds felt like a prisoner's chains, they were so heavy. Her mouth was so dry, she doubted if she could speak.

The Earl greeted her mother courteously, then without further ado came to stand beside Kate. Gently taking her hands in his, he said, 'Miss Roscoe, will you do me the very great honour of accepting my hand in marriage?'

Kate stared up into his face. His startling blue eyes seemed to blaze down into hers, powerful and mesmerising.

'Yes, I will,' she murmured, dropping her eyes to the floor as she could hardly withstand his gaze. She heard her mother let out a long sigh.

The Earl turned to Mrs Roscoe. 'Madam, I wonder if you would consider it appropriate for me to have a few words in private with Miss Roscoe?'

Mrs Roscoe hesitated. In usual circumstances this would not seem quite proper, yet she hardly dare go against the request of the Earl.

'If you would kindly step into the hallway and sit there for a few minutes, leaving the door open for propriety's sake,' the Earl suggested reassuringly. 'I'm sure that will be quite satisfactory for all parties.'

Mrs Roscoe smiled and duly left the room.

The Earl beckoned to Kate to sit with him on the small chaise longue beside the window. 'Miss Roscoe — '

'Kate,' she intercepted quietly.

He smiled. 'Kate,' he said, speaking

so softly the words were entirely private between the two of them, 'I need to explain a number of things to you as I realise you must find my offer of marriage somewhat startling, given that we have known each other for so little time.'

She nodded, biting her lip. 'Earl Gresham,' she said, determined not to be intimidated by this daunting situation, 'if you have asked me to marry you, simply in order to save me and my mother from disgrace in London society, and if you should regret that at any time before we marry, then I shall be most willing to release you from your promise.' She turned her head away from him, not wanting to reveal her true feelings.

He placed his fingers gently under her chin, turning her to look at him. 'I asked you to be my wife because I truly believe we could come to have a regard for each other, and because I admire you very much, Kate. And I believe that you will be able to offer my children the love and guiding hand of a mother. I also happen to know that the person who has been spreading stories about you is both powerful and dangerous. Which is why I decided to take matters into my own hands on your behalf; it was necessary to act immediately before any real damage could be done.'

Kate would have preferred a more passionate declaration than this — fiery words based on the notion of love and desire. She realised that this was unrealistic. She put her hand up against her throat, trying to calm herself.

'If I had not been so foolish as to get myself into this scrape, would you still have planned to ask for my hand in marriage?' she asked candidly.

'Yes, I would. But maybe not with such haste.'

'What does your sister, Lady Helen, think of all this?' she asked softly.

'She is rather startled. However, she knows that I am apt to make swift decisions, and that I am rarely mistaken in what I judge to be right.'

Some people would call him arrogant, Kate thought. But to her he seemed splendidly honest and courageous. She took away her hand from her throat, then seeing the flash of the diamonds quickly replaced it.

The Earl smiled. 'Why are you hiding your diamonds, Kate?'

'They are not mine, they are my mother's.' She returned his faintly mocking smile. 'And they are very heavy and I'd rather like to take them off.'

'Do you not like diamonds? I was of the persuasion that all young ladies liked diamonds.'

She held his gaze, giving a faint shake of her head.

'There are some very fine diamonds in the Gresham family connection,' he said. 'I was planning to give them to you.'

'That is very kind. But I think you should keep them for your little girls.'

'I shall need to ponder on that,' he said. 'And do please call me Rupert.'

We are flirting, Kate thought. *He is teasing me, and I love it. And I think I can hold my own with him.*

'Is there anything else you would like to ask me?' the Earl was asking.

She looked down. There were a hundred things, but one which really seemed to matter. 'What was the name of your late wife?' *What was she like?* she added to herself.

His eyes shimmered with feeling. 'She was called Josefa. She was a Hungarian princess. I loved her with all my heart.'

Kate began to understand what she was taking on.

Rupert Gresham took her hands in his once again. 'I think your mama will be anxiously waiting to join us. So I will simply say one last thing, and that is to make you a promise that I shall always take care of you, my dear Kate. And I shall try to make you as happy as you could possibly wish.'

I am that now, thought Kate. *I am the luckiest woman in the world.*

* * *

Two days afterwards the society ladies of London were astounded to see in The Times an announcement of the engagement of the Earl of Gresham to Miss Katherine Roscoe.

'Who is she?' everyone was asking, agog. 'Who is this unknown young lady who has walked away with the biggest prize of the London Season?' The mamas were vocal in their outrage, and the debutantes seeking a husband were permitting themselves some jealous sulking.

Mrs Roscoe read the announcement over so many times that the page nearly fell into shreds. She sent Grantley out to purchase further copies.

As if by magic, it became known that Miss Roscoe had a considerable personal fortune, and was a lady to be cultivated. A triumphant Mrs Roscoe spent her mornings sweeping around Bond Street purchasing a handsome trousseau for Kate and overseeing the progress of the bridal gown, being sewn by Madame Antoinette in person. In the afternoons, a stream of visitors passed through the drawing room of the mother of the bride-to-be.

For Kate, the days flew by in a haze of joy and anticipation. In the mornings the Earl took her driving in Hyde Park, by way of showing her off to all who were interested. In the evenings they attended balls together, but as he did not care for dancing, they simply took one turn around the floor and then he took her in to supper.

He took her to his London mansion, and there she began to make friends with his children, Lady Josefa and Lady Constance. She and her mother were invited to his sister's house, where both Lady Helen and her merchant banker husband, Hugo, welcomed them with polite cordiality.

Kate found Rupert Gresham attentive, teasing, witty, provoking and altogether everything she had ever hoped for in a man. Whilst always courteous and

admiring, he was very correct in his behaviour towards her. He always offered
her his arm when they walked out together,
but there were no snatched cuddles or
passionate kisses. There was a gentle
aloofness about him which only served
to make him more fascinating and mysterious. Kate longed for them to be
married so that they could have all the
time and privacy they needed to get to
know each other better.

A month before the wedding, the
Earl visited Coutts bank to speak to
his principal money advisor there. He
informed the man that he would require
Miss Roscoe to have complete control
of her dowry, which Mrs Roscoe would
pass on to her once Kate was a married
woman.

'But, your Grace,' the advisor protested, 'is that wise? To allow a young
woman the management of so much
money? Surely it would be more pru-
dent to restrict her control to the traditional
third.'

The Earl fixed him with his gimlet

gaze. 'Just carry out my instructions,' he replied, taking up his hat and cane and departing.

Settled later on in the library at the Athenaeum Club, he took out his pen and laid a sheet of notepaper on the desk in front of him. After some consideration he began to compose a letter to his friend, Mrs Cheveney.

4

On a hot, sunny day in July, Kate married Rupert, Earl of Gresham. It was a quiet, family occasion at the wish of the Earl in respect of his dead wife. Kate had been only too happy to go along with his gentle request for as little fuss as possible, and she herself much preferred a simple wedding.

Mrs Roscoe, thrilled as she was to witness her daughter marrying such a grandee, could not help thinking how truly wonderful it would have been to have had Kate's marriage in St Paul's or maybe the Chapel at Windsor. There could have been hundreds of illustrious guests. But she was not a lady to brood for long, and kept hugging herself with pride to watch her daughter, in a beautiful ivory dress sewn with pearls, standing at the altar with a peer of the realm. Moreover, her little indiscretion of a few weeks before was now forgotten. And when Mrs Roscoe went visiting later in the week, she could talk of 'her dear daughter, the Countess of Gresham.'

Rupert's two little girls were attendants, their chubby fingers clutching pretty nosegays of white and pink rosebuds. Kate made her responses in a clear, sweet voice, and later signed the register with a sure hand.

The wedding breakfast was held at the historic Clarendon Hotel, and afterwards the bride went to change into her going-away dress. The Earl had suggested they spend their wedding night at Claridges in Brook Street, returning to Gresham Abbey the next day. They had agreed that an extensive wedding tour abroad was not what they wished for. And Kate, in particular, was eager to get to know the Earl's main home in Derbyshire and to set about becoming a loving mother to his children.

Mrs Roscoe became tearful when the

time came to say goodbye to her daughter. Suddenly she recalled Kate as a girl, running in the gardens of their house, chasing the peacocks, clapping her hands and looking back lovingly at her watching parents. And suddenly all that mattered was that her Kate would be happy with her choice of husband. She looked at the Earl, thinking him exceedingly magnetic, recalling his pedigree and his fortune — and yet wondering if he were truly good enough for her darling girl.

Kate wrapped her arms around her mother's neck. 'You have no need to worry about me, Mama. I shall be so very happy with Rupert. Bea will keep an eye on me for you. And then in a few weeks, you must come and visit us at Gresham Abbey.'

Mrs Roscoe hugged her daughter tightly, reflecting that it was a momentous journey Kate was now embarking on; giving herself heart, body and soul to a man. A man she hardly knew. 'Be a good wife to him,' she said solemnly, ever practical and well aware of a mother's duty to give firm advice on an occasion such as this.

The Earl had booked a suite at Claridges. The sitting room was enormous and beautifully decorated in the latest style. A huge display of flowers stood in the fireplace and the fire irons surrounding it gleamed in the late evening sunshine. A bottle of champagne stood in a silver ice bucket on the gleaming mahogany table set by the window.

Rupert had ordered a light supper of cold meats and a raspberry mousse, and they sat down together to eat it. Alone at last. At her request, he talked to her about Gresham Abbey and his future plans for the estate. Kate was very interested in the house which was to be her new home, and Rupert's descriptions of it had painted a rather beautiful picture.

He laid his fork down and looked across at her. 'You look very tired, Kate,' he said. 'Would you care to retire?'

Kate swallowed, knowing that the time was drawing near when the mysteries of married love would be revealed to her. She desperately wanted to be close to Rupert, but at the same time sensed an apprehension of what was to come. Whether she would please him — whether the process would be as distasteful as she had heard some married women hint at.

'Yes, I think I would like to rest now,' she told Rupert. She got to her feet and then shyly dropped a light kiss on his cheek.

He put her hand to his lips. 'I will join you soon.' He rang the bell and a servant appeared. 'You may clear the supper things away,' Rupert told him, 'and then ask the Countess Gresham's maid to come and attend her.'

'Countess Gresham,' Kate said, smiling. 'It sounds so strange. But it's a lovely name.'

'I have always thought so,' he said dryly.

They smiled at one another and a

trembling thrill shot through Kate. She went into the bedroom, which was decorated in sumptuous velvet wall-paper and dominated by an imposing four-poster in fine floral damask.

Bea came in to help Kate get ready for bed. She unpinned her hair and began to brush it. 'How are you feeling, Miss Kate?' she asked soothingly. 'Ooh, no, I need to call you your Ladyship. Or should it be Your Grace?'

Kate laughed. 'I'm really not sure. I will have to ask my husband.'

Bea sighed in rapture. 'Your husband! Who would have thought it? And him an earl, too.'

'Don't you think I am good enough for an earl?' Kate teased.

'You are good enough for a prince, Miss Kate,' said Bea firmly. She laid Kate's nightgown on the bed, the one Mrs Roscoe had directed her to put out on the wedding night. It was a frothy confection of silk and lace, the silk so delicate it was almost sheer.

Kate gave a little gasp as it slithered

over her shoulders and hips. 'My goodness, isn't this a touch improper?'

'All the better to please your husband, Miss Kate — or Countess Kate, I should say perhaps.'

Kate smiled. Everything was beginning to seem slightly unreal.

Bea extinguished the lamp on the dressing table, leaving only the bedside candle's small glow as she crept away, closing the door softly.

The room was mainly dark now, the evening light having faded behind the curtains. Kate lay very still, listening for Rupert's footsteps. When he came in she could see only his tall, lean silhouette.

She sat up, watching him approach, her heart beating thickly.

He sat on the bed. 'You look so lovely, my dear,' he murmured. 'And so young.' He took one of the strands curling out from under her nightcap and wound it around his finger. And then he leaned forward and kissed her lips very gently. 'You don't have to be afraid, my darling,' he breathed. 'I won't do anything to hurt you — you know that, don't you?'

Kate wound her arms around his neck. He stroked his fingertips lingeringly over her face and her neck and arms. And then he kissed her, and sensations she had never felt before began to open up in her body. She closed her eyes and let the intense pleasure of moulding herself against him fill her with astonishment and delight.

★　★　★

When Rupert woke the following morning he turned to see Kate fast asleep beside him, her russet curls fanned out over the pillow, her slender white shoulder showing as a blurred outline through the silk of her nightdress. Recollections of the previous night played in his head and he felt an enormous tenderness for his new young bride, an emotion he had felt only for his children since Josefa died two years before.

Recalling Kate's complete innocence of the act of love, and the little cry she had been unable to repress as their lovemaking proceeded to its resolution, he had a sudden flash of feeling regarding his former lover Arabella Cheveney. The notion of his secret betrayal of both his charming new wife and his worldly and seductive lover made him feel shabby and selfish. Frowning, he turned back the bed-clothes, picked up his dressing gown and went into his dressing room. Once fully attired in his buttoned shirt, trousers and stiff collar, he began to feel more like his usual self.

As he pulled on his boots, he was glad that Kate had agreed with his plan to go straight to Gresham after breakfast. Once he was in his childhood home and free to roam over his acres of land, he would surely recover his self-esteem.

Kate woke, feeling wonderfully happy

and relaxed. Her hand reached out into the part of the bed Rupert had slept in and stroked it lovingly. Tiny thrills of excitement shivered like shiny silver filaments inside every vein of her body as she remembered the ways in which he had touched her, the feel of his strong, muscular body.

He was waiting in the foyer as she went down to the dining room. 'My dear,' he said, giving her a formal kiss on her cheek. 'Did you sleep well?'

She slipped her arm into his, smiling up at him. He was his usual gently aloof self again. It was as though nothing had happened between them last night. But she knew that when they were alone it would happen again, and that the prospect of his caresses, and of spending the whole day with him, was surely like having been given a foretaste of heaven.

The train was waiting for them on the platform. The bulk of Kate's luggage had been sent on the day before, so there was just her valise to be placed in the luggage compartment. Bea took charge of that and settled herself in a second-class carriage, alert in case she should be needed.

Kate noticed Rupert's children, Lady Josefa and Lady Constance, standing on the platform with their nanny, an unsmiling white-haired lady dressed in severe dark blue and wearing a white apron. The children were excited, wanting to run about the platform, but the nanny held each in a firm handclasp. Little Constance started to cry.

'Will the children travel in the carriage with us?' Kate asked, knowing the answer as soon as she registered Rupert's faintly amused expression.

'Of course not, they will be travelling with Nanny.'

Kate saw that Constance was sobbing now. Her heart went out to the child whose nanny was taking little notice of the childish protests, doing nothing to ease the little girl's distress.

Turning away, she followed Rupert

onto the train where they sat opposite each other in an ornate first class carriage. She felt the wheels begin to move as the train pulled out of the station. She tried not to dwell on little Constance's unhappiness. There would be plenty of time for her to spend time with the little girls in the future and offer them her love and understanding.

Rupert was armed for the journey with a copy of *The Times* and she with a choice of Mary Shelley's *Frankenstein* or Charles Dicken's *Little Dorritt,* both of which her mother had expressly forbidden her to read. But now she was a married woman and she could do as she pleased. She glanced across at Rupert, mischief bubbling from her smile. His lips curled slightly, an eyebrow was raised and he returned to his newspaper.

'I like the railways,' Kate said suddenly, as she watched the countryside flash by, dotted with cows and horses grazing in the fields.

'Is that so?' Rupert replied. 'And so do I. When I was a young boy I used to stand in one of our fields close to the line and wave as the train went past. I had great ambitions of becoming a driver.'

Kate laughed. 'Just think how it would feel, having all that power at your fingertips,' she said. 'It must be like taming a dragon.'

Rupert nodded and returned again to his newspaper. Kate opted for *Frankenstein*, read the opening pages and was soon totally absorbed in the novel's strange world. She read on, intent on the text, not realising that Rupert had laid aside his paper and was looking steadily at her, an unreadable expression in his eyes.

Two carriages and four coachmen were waiting for them at the station preparing to drive them the four miles to Gresham Abbey. As Rupert handed Kate down from the train, a woman with a knitted shawl tied around her frock, stepped forward with a bunch of sweet peas. Dropping a little curtsey she offered them to Kate. 'These are for you, My Lady Countess,' she said.

'This is Mrs James,' Rupert explained. 'The wife of the stationmaster.'

Kate was surprised and touched. 'Thank you, Mrs James. That is most kind of you.'

Rupert handed her into the carriage, with Bea following in attendance. The second carriage was occupied by the two little girls and their nanny.

As they drove through the village of Gresham, people were standing at their garden gates or along the dusty road. Children waved flags, and threw little posies of wild flowers into the carriage.

'Good gracious!' exclaimed Kate, glancing at Bea whose mouth had dropped open with amazement. 'It's like the arrival of the Queen of Sheba.'

'Wave back, Kate,' Rupert prompted, in cool tones. 'They are doing this especially for us — the newlyweds.'

Just outside the village, the carriage rolled under the arch of a great stone gateway and they were in a park lined with gracious beech trees. Deer and sheep grazed on the silky pasture land.

They rounded a corner and there before them was Gresham Abbey.

Kate drew in a breath. It was a most imposing building, long and U-shaped, with three storeys and an enormous arched doorway. The windows of the house were Gothic in style, giving the building a sombre, gracious air.

'The windows along the front were taken in their entirety from the old abbey,' Rupert explained. 'But the west wing was put on at a later date and you'll notice that the windows are mullioned.'

'It is all so beautiful,' Kate said, smiling at the cheeky-looking gargoyles, and then glancing east where the ruins of the old abbey stood.

'It is your home now, Kate,' Rupert said in a low, sincere voice. 'I hope you are going to be happy in it.'

Kate reached across and placed her small hand over his.

As they drew up at the entrance, the huge Gothic door opened and the butler and housekeeper stepped forward, flanked by the servants. Kate was used to servants at her mother's house but a small army such as this was somewhat daunting.

The butler stepped forward, bowing first to Rupert and then to Kate. 'Welcome, my Lady,' he said gravely to Kate, his pale blue eyes rapidly skimming her up and down.

'This is Hedges,' Rupert explained. 'He runs the house with clockwork precision.' Rupert then introduced her to Mrs Priestley, the housekeeper, a tall stately woman around forty, dressed all in black.

'I think I shall need your help, Mrs Priestley,' Kate told the impressive servant. 'I'm not accustomed to a house this size.'

Mrs Priestley dropped a curtsey. 'I shall be most pleased to assist you in any way you require, My Lady Countess,' she said formally.

Kate had a worried feeling that Mrs Priestley fancied she might have Kate for breakfast, Lady Countess or not. She would need to watch her step.

'Mrs Priestley will show you to your room, my dear,' Rupert said to Kate. 'No doubt you will want to rest for a while after the journey. I look forward to seeing you at dinner.'

And then he turned away, and began talking to a man dressed in thick tweeds whom Kate guessed was his estates manager.

Trying to ignore a sinking feeling of being abandoned, Kate beckoned to Bea and followed Mrs Priestley up the great oak staircase. Her bedroom was light and airy with a four-poster curtained in pretty chintz and a beautiful Chinese carpet.

Mrs Priestley showed her the wardrobes and dressers, then indicated a door in the centre of one of the side walls. 'This leads to the Earl's dressing room, with an adjoining door to his bedroom,' she explained.

'Thank you,' said Kate, feeling herself blush at the prospect of Rupert's closeness to her during the hours of darkness and of receiving him into her bed again that night.

'Tea will be served at four o'clock in the yellow drawing room, my lady,' Mrs Priestley announced. 'Or if you prefer I could have a tray sent to your personal sitting room in the West Wing.'

'I'll come down to the yellow drawing room,' Kate said firmly.

Mrs Priestley curtsied again, then made a majestic exit, leaving Kate and Bea to exchange meaningful glances.

'What a grand place this is,' Bea exclaimed. 'I wonder where that dragon is going to put me. I hope it's not too far away. I need to keep an eye on you, my lady, make sure you're happy.'

Kate smiled. 'I will be fine once I settle in — and so will you, Bea. There aren't many things that can intimidate you!'

'Huh, Miss Kate, and a good thing too! All this bowing and scraping and putting on airs. I'm not sure I care for it.'

Kate raised her eyebrows. Bea's face crumpled in apology. 'Oh, I don't mean you and the Earl. He's a real gentleman and deserves all the respect due to him. And so do you, Miss Kate. My lady.'

Kate gave Bea one of her warmest smiles and let out a sigh of mock relief. 'Well, that's all right then!'

Changed from her travelling attire into a simple frock of cream cotton lawn, Kate presented herself in the yellow drawing room at the appointed hour. Hedges was on hand to receive her at the bottom of the staircase and show her into the drawing room. The tea was already set out. A small silver tea service was placed on a table beside one of the two splendid sofas beside the fireplace. There was a little feast of bread and butter, a pot of jam, tiny sandwiches and slices of cherry cake set out on silver dishes. And just one china cup, saucer and plate placed on the snow white tablecloth.

'Do you require anything further, Countess Gresham?' the butler enquired solemnly.

'No thank you, Hedges,' she said,

thinking that the formal Hedges was very like Grantley at her mother's house. Which was quite a comfort.

Hedges glided silently away and Kate felt herself utterly alone in this vast, charming, but rather forbidding room. She poured herself tea and wandered about the room, looking at the fine china vases and the brooding paintings depicting darkened landscapes featuring stags with huge antlers. Over the mantelpiece was portrait of a man she guessed to be one of Rupert's forbears, the facial features were so like those of her husband.

After fifteen minutes, she found herself tiring of solitude and rang the bell.

Hedges appeared almost instantly. 'You rang, Countess Gresham.'

Kate smiled at his sombre features. 'I'd like to visit the nursery,' she said.

There was a tiny pause. 'Of course, Ma'am, please follow me.'

They made their way up the main staircase, passing the ascending gallery of more family portraits, then turned in the opposite direction from Kate's bedroom. They proceeded along a corridor and eventually mounted a half flight of steps. Hedges knocked softly on the door at the top, allowed a few seconds to pass, then opened the door and went in.

The nanny was sitting beside the window reading a book. When she saw Kate, she started to her feet, a faintly guilty expression on her stern features. 'Your Ladyship,' she said, curtseying.

Kate saw that the nanny was quite old, perhaps in her mid-sixties. She sensed an atmosphere of tension and unease in the big, airy room.

The nanny smoothed down her white apron. 'How can I help you, ma'am?' she asked.

'I have come to see my husband's children,' Kate said, aiming to sound friendly and yet make the nanny very conscious of her position as the new mistress of this great household.

The nanny gave a little cough. 'Of course, ma'am.'

'Where are they?' Kate asked.

'They are taking a nap, ma'am. I will go and prepare them to see you.'

Kate sensed something furtive in the woman's manner. 'There is no need to prepare them,' she said, smiling, yet firm. 'Just bring them to see me.'

The nanny opened a door leading from the main nursery to the children's bedroom. She slipped quickly through and closed the door behind her.

Kate frowned, deliberating on what she should do. She moved forward and softly opened the door, instantly sizing up the situation. The two little girls were sitting in high-sided cots, watching warily as the nanny approached them. Both their faces were pink and streaked with tears, and it seemed they had no toys to play with or books to look at. They were dressed in their night-time clothes.

Hearing the footsteps behind her, the nanny turned, her face a set mask betraying no readable emotion.

Kate smiled at the two little girls.

'Come along,' she said encouragingly, 'let's go and find some toys to play with.'

In the children's suspiciously tidy playroom, she opened the big wooden toy box and took out building bricks, skittles, soft balls and some picture books made of linen which appeared pristine and unused.

As the children seemed something at a loss to know what they should do with the toys, Kate sat on the floor with them and began to build a small tower from the bricks. The little girls watched, wide-eyed. Kate placed a small pile of bricks in front of each child. She gently knocked down her own little pile and then suggested they should all build a new one together. It took some minutes to achieve the three small towers as the children seemed apprehensive about handling the bricks. But after they had built and knocked down several towers, they began to relax. Kate picked up one of the balls and rolled it to Josefa. She squealed with delight as it bounced against her leg, then carefully picked it up and rolled it back to Kate.

When the nanny came in with their undergarments, both children instantly became still and solemn. At the woman's request they stood rigidly whilst their clothes were put on. When their glances slid to Kate, she smiled. Her heart went out to them.

'We only play with one toy at a time,' the nanny said stiffly, picking up most of the toys and returning them to the box. 'It teaches them to be tidy and also to concentrate on one thing.' Her beady glance was letting Kate know that she, not the lady of the house, was queen bee in the nursery.

Kate decided that diplomacy was the best strategy for the moment, even though all her instincts were to put this dragon-like woman in her place and institute a completely new regime in the nursery with immediate effect. 'Well, then,' she said, smiling at the children, 'why don't we choose a book and read it together?'

Soon she was sitting with a child on each side of her, looking through a picture book of farm animals. The time seemed to fly by as she read and talked and then sang to her two little step-daughters. Happiness flowed through her, easing the occasional feelings of isolation and uncertainty she had experienced earlier in the day.

At five o'clock the door opened and a maid came in with a large tray. There were sandwiches, game pie, muffins and cakes for the nanny. And for the children, two bowls of grey-looking porridge and some thick white blancmange.

'Go and wash your hands,' the nanny told them, 'then sit at your table.'

The two went off like little clockwork mice, returning to sit at a low table on child-sized chairs. The nanny wound napkins around each of their necks. 'Put your hands together and close your eyes,' she said, before reciting a thank-you to God for what they were about to receive. 'Eat your supper.'

The nanny stood watching the children,

in a rigidly supervisory manner. Kate, in turn, was unashamedly appraising the older woman, noticing her frequent longing looks at her own supper laid out on the polished adult table. She was also aware of the children's reluctance to eat up their revolting-looking tea.

'Why are the children not eating their food?' she asked the nanny, her tone gentle, her eyes demanding an answer.

'Perhaps they are not hungry.' The nanny's expression was mutinous.

'What did they have for lunch?' Kate enquired.

'Soup and then some jelly.'

It occurred to Kate that the nanny was still giving these two growing children baby food. That could not be right. She had quite a lot of experience with children, having regularly visited her former housemaid after she was married and had two children. 'Perhaps they would like to try a sandwich,' she said, looking across at the nanny's plate.

The woman bristled now, her eyes

filled with a cold anger.

'I suggest they could try one each,' Kate said, noting that the children were listening in with fascination to this dialogue.

Frowning, the nanny placed two egg sandwiches on a plate. The girls' eyes glistened with anticipation, but they held back from touching the food.

Kate smiled. 'Go ahead and eat your sandwiches.' She realised she was undermining the nanny. But at that moment, the children's plight seemed more urgent than any consideration for the older woman's feelings.

The children wolfed down the sandwiches and looked up hopefully.

'There are no more egg ones,' the nanny said. 'The rest are meat and not at all suitable for babies.'

'Then I'll send down to the kitchen for some more egg ones,' Kate said, making an effort to keep her tone pleasant. She picked up the little brass bell on the table and gave it several brisk rings.

What am I going to do? she asked herself. She could not stand by and let the children suffer any more under the regime of this elderly nanny. But for the time being, she stayed whilst the children ate their sandwiches, and promised she would be back to give them a goodnight kiss.

Later on, as she dressed for dinner, she planned how she might approach Rupert on the issue of the children's care, knowing that she would need to be very diplomatic. They were, after all, his children, not hers. But she was beginning to love them, just as she loved him.

5

Whilst Kate was engaged in the nursery wing, Rupert had ridden over to Cheveney Court. On arriving, he dismounted and handed his horse to a footman, who had come out with the butler to meet him.

'Good afternoon, Earl Gresham,' the butler said with cordial formality. 'If you would like to wait in the drawing room, I will advise Mrs Cheveney of your arrival.'

Rupert sighed as the butler withdrew, aware that the servant knew very well what the relationship had been between himself and Arabella Cheveney. He would, of course, be entirely reliable about keeping the information to himself, but when Rupert thought of his innocent and lovely young wife, he felt a pang of regret for his past dalliance.

Sitting in her boudoir, Arabella was

thrown into a panic of alarm and delight when she heard that her lover had arrived. She rang furiously for her maid and set about stripping off her grey muslin gown in order to change into a dress of deep pink silk, which clung in soft folds around her figure.

'Come along, hurry up, you silly girl!' she chided her maid, as the girl did up the tiny silk-covered buttons. When she was at last ready, she waved the maid away impatiently and surveyed herself in the mirror, admiring the curve of her full breasts and the smallness of her waist.

Arabella Cheveney was not a woman to take no for an answer, and whilst Rupert's letter had been quite clear on the point of the need to terminate their relationship, she did not believe that he truly meant it. From what she had heard, his new wife was a skinny, freckled redhead from nowhere, who had obviously set her cap at the prize of a rich aristocrat such as Rupert, Earl of Gresham. But how could such a girl satisfy a man as sophisticated and worldly as Earl Gresham, as she, Arabella had done? And as she intended to continue doing once the gloss of his re-marriage had worn off.

She had always been an ambitious woman. Ten years ago she had been pleased to accept an offer of marriage from the enormously wealthy Gerald Cheveney, twenty-five years her senior. He, in turn, had been delighted to win the most beautiful debutante of the season. But the excitement of luxury and lavish spending had faded for Arabella. Once her husband reached his mid-fifties, suffered cruelly from gout and was no longer able to please his wife in the bedroom, she had decided she needed entertainment.

It had taken her some time to seduce the grieving Earl of Gresham after his wife's death, but it had been the most exciting project of her life. The Earl, in addition to his excellent aristocratic pedigree, was charismatic, knowledge-able and cultured. He was also a most considerate and skilful lover. He was a prize not to be given up. And now, even though he was once again married, she was determined to fight in order to keep him.

The butler had left the drawing room door slightly ajar and Arabella could see Rupert standing by the window, looking out over the park, his hands behind his back, his face hawk-like and impartial. She felt a jolt of unease, wondering what her tactics should be in ensuring that their old relationship might be resumed as soon as possible.

She put up a hand to pat her golden ringlets, before walking forward into the drawing room and stretching out her arms.

'My dearest,' she said, keeping her voice soft and low, 'I am so sorry to have kept you waiting.' She turned her cheek for him to kiss.

Rupert gave a faint smile and touched her cheek lightly with the tips of his fingers. Arabella felt another little jolt, suddenly sensing that things were not going to be as easy as she had imagined.

'Arabella,' Rupert said quietly, 'it has come to my notice that rumours have been spreading about the Countess.' He had, in fact, heard from Lady Helen that Arabella been making less than complimentary comments about the little girl from the North who had bagged herself a title. And that she had also made allusions to the incident in Piccadilly.

Arabella flinched and a deep blush crept up her neck. This was the very last thing she had expected. She swallowed hard, putting her hands up to her face, trying desperately to prevent him seeing her discomfiture.

'I am sorry to hear that,' she told him. She recalled the conversation at the Walton's dinner party; Lord Walton's story of Kate Roscoe's outing.

It had all been so delicious to hear. She had listened with breathless interest, and it had been impossible to keep total silence on the matter. After all, one had to have something to relate when one went calling on one's friends. But she had been very discreet, hadn't she? Surely she had only dropped hints, and then only once or twice.

She straightened her shoulders and met Rupert's steady, quizzical gaze. 'I hope you are not accusing me of being a party to such tittle-tattle,' she said with as much dignity as she could manage.

'In no way am I accusing you of anything,' he said. 'Naturally the Countess is now under my protection, and I shall have no hesitation in taking action on her behalf, should that seem necessary.' He paused to let the words sink in.

'Of course,' Arabella said. She glanced at him, wishing that she could be close to him once more, bask in the joy of his presence and his love-making.

'I must apologise for any distress my letter might have caused you,' he said. 'I felt it was only courteous to call and speak to you in person.'

She stared at him, her mouth drying.

It was as though he were gently pulling the rug from beneath her dainty feet.

'I am most appreciative of our former friendship,' he went on. 'Your companionship meant a lot to me following the loss of my dear first wife.'

'Thank you,' Arabella said, smiling, yet still hoping to find a way to inject warmth into this cool exchange. 'I look forward to meeting your new wife. Gerald and I would be delighted to receive you both for dinner, or maybe a weekend visit?'

There was a short silence.

'Arabella,' he said, 'there will be no visiting in future between Cheveney Court and Gresham Abbey. I am sorry.'

Arabella gazed at him in shock and panic. 'Rupert!' she exclaimed.

'I regret telling you this,' he said. 'But you must understand that life has changed for me, now that I have married again. I am sure you will appreciate that I owe my new Countess all the courtesy due to her position.'

Arabella flung a hand across her

heart. Oh, that really hurt! To think of that little chit of a girl being afforded all this respect and consideration!

She did not know with whom she was most angry. With her old impotent husband for not conveniently dying so that she could have married Rupert and become his Countess? Or that little upstart, Kate Roscoe, who had dashed all her hopes and arrived at the winning post, having hardly run the race at all? Or, of course, with Rupert himself — who was tossing away her, one of society's greatest beauties, like an old glove?

She clenched her hands and willed herself to behave with calm and dignity. All might not be lost. Rupert could soon tire of a shallow young wife. And in time Arabella could step in once again and play the role of comforting mistress. She smoothed her hands over her shapely hips and reminded herself of how desirable she was. He would come round — oh yes, she was sure of it.

'Are you planning to go on a honeymoon journey?' she asked, making her tone sweet and low.

'The Countess and I have decided to stay at home for a time. She wishes to get to know my children, a project of which I highly approve.'

Damn the darling little Countess, thought Arabella, who could not stand the company of little children and considered that they should be neither seen nor heard. She returned to the main subject of their conversation.

'My dear Rupert,' she said, in regal tones, 'I do so appreciate your coming to speak to me personally. It is a demonstration of the depth of our friendship — and, dare I say it? — our love. And whilst I understand that you do not feel it appropriate for my husband and me to become acquainted with the new Countess, let me assure you that you and she will always be welcome, should you wish to call at Cheveney Manor.'

With that, she gave him a long look

from beneath her eyelashes, reached up and kissed his cheek, then made what she considered a most timely and affecting exit, walking gracefully through the door and then closing it gently behind her.

But by the time Rupert had left the house and she had reached the privacy of her boudoir, she had lost all her composure and was shedding hot tears of rage and despair. The notion of the new Countess of Gresham glorying in all her new triumphs was simply too much to bear. She reached into a drawer for her flask of brandy, took a few sips and then sat down at her desk, biting her lips and drumming her fists on the delicate cherry wood.

Arabella was not a woman given to calm, reflective thinking, but she was good at hatching plots. In time she got out her pen, drew a sheet of paper towards her and began to write.

★ ★ ★

Over dinner that night, as they ate roast duck and baby potatoes, Kate decided it was time to raise the issue of the Earl's children. She laid down her knife and fork and took a sip of the excellent claret that had been brought up from the Gresham wine cellar.

'I took my tea with the children today,' she informed him brightly.

He looked across at her. 'Ah, yes. How kind of you. They're not used to many visitors in the nursery,' he commented.

'I'd like them to get to know me, so that I don't seem like a visitor,' Kate said with gentle meaningfulness.

He smiled. 'Of course, my dear Kate. That is what I would wish, too.'

There was a tiny silence.

'How did you find them?' Rupert asked.

'Delightful,' Kate answered. 'They are lovely children.'

'But?' he said, levelling one of his deep gazes at her.

Kate took a breath. 'But I was wondering if perhaps I could make a few suggestions about their diet and

. . . their routine?'

'Of course,' Rupert said, easily. 'You are the mistress of this house, Kate. If you wish Nanny to make some alterations or improvements in their regime, then by all means go ahead and inform her.'

This is too easy, thought Kate. *And at the same time curiously difficult.*

'But they are your children, Rupert. Don't you wish to have a say?'

He raised his eyebrows. 'My dear, they are only two and a half years of age, mere babies. As a father I don't feel I have any qualifications for making decrees about their management at this early stage.'

Kate longed to ask what role the children's mother had taken, but hesitated to do so. It also struck her that the children were very young at the time of her death, so maybe the situation had been very different. She felt his eyes on her as he awaited her response.

She took another sip of wine and Hedges, who had been standing by, walked forward to top up her glass. Reminded of the butler's silent presence she could not bring herself to talk frankly. There was another silence.

'Nanny looked after me and my sister Helen when we were babies. She has been in the family for forty or so years,' Rupert said, helping her out.

'Oh, I see.' Kate began to see that she had a real problem on her hands in terms of dealing with Nanny.

Rupert smiled reassuringly. 'Just tell Nanny that I have every faith in your recommendations for the children.'

'Yes,' she said, taking up her knife and fork again and spearing a potato.

'My dear, did you bring your violin to Gresham?' Rupert enquired kindly.

She looked up, surprised at this turn in the conversation, as though the previous one was of limited importance and all done and dusted.

'Yes, I did.'

'Splendid. Will you play for me after dinner?'

She nodded. And no more was said about the children or their nanny.

* * *

The next day Rupert received a letter from his sister, Lady Helen, who was still in London. On reading the contents, he uttered some soft curses under his breath, then called for his butler and asked him to make a reservation on the next London train.

He then went to find Kate who was in the yellow drawing room, reading a letter from her mother which was full of instructions regarding what that lady considered to be the duties of the mistress of a large, noble stately home.

'My dear, am I disturbing you?' he asked, standing in the doorway.

Kate looked up and smiled at him. His presence always sent a thrill of pleasure rushing down her spine. His gentle aloofness during the days and his passionate love-making at night were a heady cocktail for a young bride. Watching him now, she wanted to run to him and place her arms around him, but she sensed that this would somehow not be quite proper and that he might not welcome such a spontaneous show of affection at this hour and in this rather public place. 'No, of course you are not disturbing me.'

'I have to go to London on business.'

'I see,' she said, disappointed and a little apprehensive that he was going to leave her to her own devices in the grandeur of Gresham Abbey. 'Will you return in time for dinner?' she asked.

'I hope so, my dear. But if I am very late, please go ahead and dine without me. Hedges will look after you.'

She nodded and forced a smile. He crossed quickly to her chair, dropped a light kiss on the top of her head, turned around — and was gone.

'Oh, goodness!' Kate exclaimed to herself as she stood at the window, watching him walk out to the carriage which had been brought round to the front door. 'What do I do now?'

She looked at her mother's letter. There were all kinds of words of advice, mainly on the subject of taking a firm hand with the domestic and kitchen staff and ensuring that there was no slacking, no idleness and most certainly no stealing. So, there was plenty to do!

Kate thought of the formidable Mrs Priestley and grimaced. And then she thought of the nanny and her face stilled into seriousness. *I do indeed have work to do today,* she told herself. She went upstairs to her room, washed her face, had Bea dress her hair in a simple but elegantly sculpted chignon, then made her way downstairs to the servants' quarters.

Walking through the servant's day quarters, she eventually found the large kitchen and stood hesitantly in the doorway for a moment.

Mrs Priestley and the nanny were sitting at the big dining table which ran the length of one side of the room. A maid was pouring coffee for them. A large oval plate holding a variety of sandwiches, cakes, and buttered scones was placed before them. Next to the food stood an open bottle of port.

The two older ladies were busy in conversation, but as the young kitchen maid nodded to them, turning her eyes to the doorway, they both jumped up, expressions of surprise and alarm on their faces.

Kate felt her heart bumping in her chest. She reminded herself that she was the wife of Rupert, Earl Gresham, and the mistress of this house.

'Please, sit down,' she told the two shocked-looking women.

Both of them remained standing stiff and upright like soldiers on parade. As Kate walked forward Mrs Priestley hurried towards her, giving a little curtsey as she halted in front of her new mistress. 'Your ladyship,' she murmured. 'We were not expecting you.'

'I'm trying to familiarise myself with the household,' Kate said, aiming to sound pleasant and yet authoritative. She racked her brains for what to say next, trying to recall her mother's methods of ordering provisions. 'I should like to go through the menus for the next day or two,' she said.

'Of course, ma'am,' Mrs Priestley said. 'The former Countess used to request me to draw up suggestions and then she would peruse them later.' She made it sound as if this was a procedure that required no alteration.

Kate wondered if this was a ploy to get her to go away and leave the two women to enjoy their coffee and substantial snacks in peace. Looking from one to the other, it occurred to her that maybe these women had something to hide. They both looked uneasy. Shifty, her mother would have called it.

'I see,' she said, smiling, whilst frantically wondering what to say next. 'Perhaps you will be kind enough to show me the pantry,' she suggested, 'so I can see what kinds of food you are accustomed to keeping in stock.'

Mrs Priestley's eyes swivelled nervously from side to side. 'Er, we don't have much in stock at the moment, ma'am,' she said. 'The master has been away for so long. Perhaps this isn't the best time to make an inspection.'

Kate's faint suspicions were now strongly aroused. 'Oh, please don't worry about that, Mrs Priestley. Just show me where the pantry is.'

The housekeeper's face was grim as she gestured to Kate to follow her from the kitchen into a large, cool room clad in bricks and furnished with thick stone shelves topped with wooden-framed food containers, some of them with wire mesh doors. Kate's eyes sped over the shelves. They looked reasonably well-stocked as far as she could tell. There were meats and vegetables, fruits, bread, cheese, bottles of chutney and sweet preserves.

'It all looks very satisfactory,' Kate remarked.

'Thank you, ma'am,' Mrs Priestley said gravely.

Kate noticed that Mrs Priestley had positioned herself at one end of the shelves and had stood there like a statue, not moving at all. Intuitively she glanced down and saw the edge of a wicker basket peeping from Mrs Priestley's voluminous skirt.

'Have you something special in the basket?' Kate asked pleasantly.

'No, ma'am.'

'You sound rather mysterious,' Kate joked. 'Do please let me see.' She walked forward and at the point where she and Mrs Priestley were about to bump into each other, the housekeeper had no choice but to move aside.

Behind her skirts was a small wicker hamper containing a leg of lamb, a side of gammon and some jars of pickles and jam. On the side of the hamper was a label with the name *Priestley* written on it in neat printing.

Realisation of what this meant raced through Kate's mind, making her nerves tingle. This senior member of the household was stealing provisions from the Gresham kitchen. She opened her mouth to speak, and then checked herself. She must be careful. There could be another explanation for what she had discovered, although she found it difficult to think what that might be. But glancing at Mrs Priestley's flaming cheeks and horrified expression, any doubts as to the woman's culpability vanished. It was as though the words 'thief caught red-handed' were written all over her face.

Kate felt the need to run upstairs and shut herself in somewhere quiet where she could decide how to proceed. But she also had a sense that it was important not to leave the two women together to cook up some kind of story. This matter needed to be dealt with now.

Feeling a weight of responsibility sitting on her shoulders like a heavy sack of logs, she straightened her spine, looked Mrs Priestley directly in the eyes and asked her to return to the kitchen.

'Mrs Priestley,' she said to the housekeeper, keeping her voice steady even though her heart was thundering in her chest, 'I would like you to tell me where the hamper I have just seen is bound for.'

There was a long pause.

'It's not what you think, ma'am,' Mrs Priestley said stiffly.

'That is not what I asked you,' Kate said firmly.

'These are items I have purchased for my family's use,' Mrs Priestley answered. Both she and the nanny were now looking sulky and mutinous as though deeply wronged by Kate's insinuations.

Kate's brain whirred into action again. *Think, think,* she told herself.

'Would you fetch the appropriate accounts book, Mrs Priestley?' she requested quietly. The housekeeper pursed her lips and went away, returning with a large black ledger.

Kate opened the book. The various items were neatly set down, together with their cost. The total arrived at for the past month was underlined in black. Kate was aware that there would only have been a skeleton staff in residence at Gresham Abbey in Rupert's absence and she knew that the amount of food ordered was far more than would have been necessary for the number of mouths to feed.

'Where are the separate entries for the food in the hampers?' she asked the housekeeper, who was now looking distinctly frightened.

There was total silence.

'I can only assume that your intention was for the Earl, your employer, to foot the bill for these items,' Kate asserted, knowing she was right.

Mrs Priestley made no response. Guilt hung in the air like grey fog.

Kate sighed. 'What about this port?' she asked, nodding in the direction of the open bottle.

'It was a Christmas present from his Lordship,' Mrs Priestley responded swiftly. 'He gives us each a bottle every year. You can ask him, ma'am.'

'Very well.' Kate was inclined to believe the housekeeper on this particular issue. Then she had another thought. Her eyes swivelled towards the nanny. 'Who is looking after the children in your absence?' she asked.

The woman bit down on her lip and bowed her head.

'If I went upstairs to look, would I find them confined in their cots?' Kate enquired, her voice laced with menace at the thought of the treatment being meted out to those two innocent children. 'Well?' she demanded.

'Yes, ma'am,' the nanny muttered.

'What are you going to do, my lady?' Mrs Priestley burst out suddenly.

'I shall have to consider,' Kate said carefully. 'But what I can tell you now is that if you make a free confession about the wrongdoings you have committed, then I will be much more inclined to leniency.

'I will give you an hour to think about it,' she concluded. 'In the meantime I shall bring the children downstairs into the yellow drawing room and care for them myself.'

She got and walked slowly from the room, every inch the Countess Gresham. The two servants looked at one another in consternation.

As she returned to the great hallway, Hedges handed her the morning post, arranged on a silver tray. The envelopes were all for Rupert, apart from one addressed to her. She looked at the writing on the envelope — bold capitals in a hand she had never seen before. Frowning, she opened it.

KEEP A WATCH ON YOUR HUSBAND, DEAR COUNTESS. YOU HAVE HIS HAND, BUT ANOTHER HAS HIS HEART.

There were just those few words. But they were enough to set Kate's nerves reeling with shock, and just a hint of sickening fear.

6

Lady Helen allowed her brother to drink his tea and consume a cucumber sandwich and a muffin before burdening him with the news she had sketched out in her letter. In her prettily furnished drawing room, the sun threw daggers of golden light onto the carpet through the tall windows. Into this atmosphere of peace, Lady Helen dropped her little bombshell.

'Rupert,' she said, 'things are even worse than I thought.'

Rupert sat back in his chair and crossed his long legs. 'Go on, my dear.'

'That nasty little toad Algernon Walton is all set to cause a horrid scandal and then sit back admiring his efforts.'

Rupert reflected that his sister liked to create an atmosphere of tension by drawing out the delivery of unwelcome information. He knew that Lady Helen was a very intelligent woman and it had often saddened him that she had had little option but to live the life of a lady of leisure. Of course, there was the running of a household to occupy her, and her charity work. But those did not really offer satisfaction. Unfortunate enough not to bear children, she was deprived of the concerns of bringing up a family. And so she had a tendency for intrigue, and sometimes a liking for exaggeration.

'Details, please,' he said. 'And there is no need to spare me the worst.'

'Well,' Lady Helen said, 'he is going around informing all and sundry that your Kate has a dubious past.'

Rupert sighed. That did not sound like good news and merited further enquiries. 'All and sundry,' he repeated. 'Who exactly?'

Lady Helen arched her eyebrows. 'My friend Lady Follett, for one.'

So maybe it was just the one, rather than all and sundry, Rupert thought. 'That puppy Algie Walton is in the habit of holding conversations with Lady Follett?' he queried dryly.

'No,' Lady Helen agreed with some sharpness. 'But he is on good terms with her son, Adolphus.'

'Ah — young bucks who like to gamble at the whist tables and drink far into the night at those London clubs which put themselves out to encourage such foolishness?'

'Yes,' said Lady Helen. 'You really shouldn't make light of this, Rupert.'

'I assure you, I'm taking what you say very seriously,' he countered. 'What exactly do you think Walton means to do to stir up a scandal?'

'His father, the duke, has friends in the publishing world,' Lady Helen explained. 'I am speaking of the newspapers, not books.'

Rupert frowned. 'So is the idea to persuade one of the major papers to print an article about my wife's so-called misdemeanour in Piccadilly?'

'Partly . . . ' As Lady Helen's voice trailed away into silence Rupert's eyes narrowed with conjecture.

'There is more?'

'Sadly, that is the case. You were seen leaving Arabella Cheveney's house the last time you visited.' She eyed him with the severity an older sister feels entitled to express. 'Which, I might add, was very recently, and subsequent to your marriage to Kate.' She shook her head in disbelief.

Rupert closed his eyes and sighed. 'I needed to speak to Arabella to make it quite clear that our liaison was over. She didn't seem to have fully understood my letter.'

'Yes, I can believe it. Arabella is not used to bowing her pretty head in respect of requests which are distasteful to her. She simply ignores them.'

'Yes, indeed,' he agreed.

'Now do you see why I am concerned?' Lady Helen demanded.

He nodded.

'Does Kate know about your relationship with Arabella?' He shook his head. 'And I presume you would not wish her to find out via some salacious comments in a newspaper?'

Rupert considered for a few moments. 'I shall go and see Walton without delay. Let's hope he's in London and not out in the country somewhere chasing furry creatures. I'm not in the mood for sitting on an edgy hunter and chasing through muddy fields after foolish cubs of the human variety.'

'You may like to know that I have been making some enquiries,' Lady Helen announced. 'Very discreetly, of course. And I think you will most likely find young Lord Walton at his favourite club. Which is the Beargarden, situated on a small side street off St James Street.'

Rupert was impressed. 'Thank you. You know, my dear Helen, you have missed your way. You would have made an excellent spy,' he told her, bending down to kiss her cheek, and then departing with all haste.

★ ★ ★

The Beargarden club was small and comfortable rather than grand, priding itself on its service, its food and its ability to cater to the needs of idle young men who liked to drink the nights away playing cards.

Rupert allowed the doorman to relieve him of his hat, and made his way through the dining room and billiard rooms to reach the card tables. At eight o'clock in the evening, the place was rather quiet. Many young men stayed on until six in the morning, then went home to sleep, not rising until the early afternoon. The tables did not really get going until approaching midnight.

However he soon spotted young Lord Walton, along with his chum, Adolphus Follett, fondly known as Dolly, playing whist with two other young fellows. They were all sitting in a haze of cigar smoke, through which Rupert could see the occasional glint of coins stacked in the middle of the table.

Rupert walked up to the slouching, half-drunk group and waited until his presence was noted. This did not take long, and Lord Walton's eyes narrowed through the smoke when he recognised the dark figure of the earl.

'A word with you, Algie,' Rupert said. He spoke softly, but the underlying tone of his voice had young Algie Walton on his feet in seconds.

'I say, Gresham, I'm a bit tied up at the moment,' Walton protested.

'I'm sure your friends can spare you for a few minutes,' Rupert told him. 'Shall we find somewhere a little quieter?' He gestured to Lord Walton to follow him, and the two made their way to one of the quieter little snugs.

'So what brings you here?' Lord Walton demanded.

'Your apparent liking for spreading slander about my Countess,' Rupert said evenly.

Walton blinked. 'By Jove! You don't beat about the bush, Gresham.'

'No,' Rupert agreed. 'So what have you to say on the matter?' He took a long cigarette from a silver case with the Gresham crest on it, lit it, and drew in the smoke. He stretched out his long legs, settled back and waited.

'A load of poppycock,' Walton said, deciding to have a shot at blustering his way through what was looking like a tricky exchange.

'So, you haven't been telling all and sundry that the Countess was seen coming out of the lodgings of a young man, holding his arm? Nor that the circumstances seemed . . . dubious?'

'What do you think I am?' Walton demanded, two red spots leaping into his cheeks.

'It is hard for me to say,' Rupert told him. 'So, did you or didn't you?'

Walton considered. 'No,' he said firmly.

'I asked you two questions,' Rupert said. 'Which are you answering?'

Walton was caught on the back foot. He was also, whilst not hopelessly drunk, at that stage when his brain was somewhat befuddled with alcohol. 'Now look here, Gresham. I think it's a bit of a nerve to beard a fellow in his den, so to speak, and make accusations against him.'

'But are they true, Algie?'

Walton bit his lip. 'I wasn't the only one who saw what happened. Ask any of my pals. In fact, why are you hounding me when I could be perfectly innocent in this matter?'

'Because I happen to know from a very reliable source that you are not innocent. You have been making insinuations about the Countess; you have been trying to blacken her name. I believe you have been bragging that you will see to it that this sorry matter reaches the newspapers.'

'All right, then,' Walton said, flaring up. 'Have it your own way. But why don't we turn the tables? Why don't we consider your motives in visiting the lovely Arabella Cheveney, only days after you married Miss Roscoe?' He allowed a smile of triumph to spread over his face. 'I know all about that. From a very reliable source who will bear witness if necessary.'

Rupert took a long pull at his cigarette. 'So, at last we come to the heart of the matter, don't we, Algie?'

'Do we?' the younger man answered insolently.

'It is your wish to get back at me that is entertaining you. Nothing to do with the former Miss Kate Roscoe who turned you down at Mrs Follett's ball. Isn't that right?'

'Oh, I wouldn't be too sure,' Walton shot back, gaining fresh confidence. 'The facts regarding your wife's conduct in Piccadilly speak for themselves. And in my view, the public has every right to know the truth about jumped-up heiresses. She is fair game.'

With a great effort, Rupert held himself back from dragging the young man out of his chair and knocking him to the ground.

'It is actually your little peccadillo with Mrs Cheveney which interests me, Gresham,' Walton drawled. 'Given that you fancy yourself as a gentleman who holds all the moral high ground.' The young fellow rolled his cigar around his mouth and grinned, enjoying his moment of triumph.

Rupert gave an internal sigh, recalling that Algie Walton had an old score to settle with him. And that he, Rupert, had unwittingly presented him with the opportunity to do exactly that.

'It would be so enjoyable to make a fellow like you squirm a bit,' Algie Walton observed. 'You with your speeches in the House of Lords about the downtrodden and the poor and women's rights.' He spat the words out, his face twisted in disdain. 'You're such a damned high-minded do-gooder.'

'And you are a low-minded ne'er-do-well,' Rupert responded bitterly. He recalled how two years before, Walton had forced his attentions on one of the kitchen maids at Gresham Abbey. The girl had undergone the humiliation of carrying a child, and had almost died giving birth. Of course it had only been her word against Walton's, and no way would a Duke's son own up to a little laddish sport and get himself into trouble. But Rupert had not let matters rest; he had forced the young man to make a handsome settlement on the girl and the child. Walton had been humiliated and outraged — and he was not a man to forgive.

'My wife is innocent of any of the insinuations you might wish to make,' Rupert said to Walton, in low steady tones. 'She does not deserve to pay for wrongs I may have done to you in the past.'

'But, Gresham,' Walton pointed out, 'if all I do is to spill the beans about your visit to Mrs Cheveney, then I am quite innocent of an attack on your wife.' He eyed Rupert like a snake ready to bite. 'And I am sure you will have been quite open with her about your liaison with Mrs Cheveney. Your wife will surely forgive you for a little extra publicity.'

'I can only appeal to you as a gentleman to refrain from publishing any information affecting either my wife or Mrs Cheveney,' Rupert said coldly.

'Too late, my dear fellow,' Walton drawled. 'It will be going to press at this very moment.' He smiled, so pleased with himself that Rupert leapt from his chair, dragged Walton from his own seat and shook him like a dog worrying a rat. He flung the young aristocrat to the ground with some force.

As he strode from the room there was a modicum of satisfaction in seeing the cocky Algie Walton flat on his back, legs flailing like those of an overturned beetle.

Consulting his watch he saw that he had missed the late train bound northwards. He had no option but to stay in London for the night. He considered returning to his sister's house, then decided that he was in no mood for explanations and discussions, even with dear Helen. It would be better to stay the night at Claridges. He hailed a cab, his heart heavy at the thought of what might transpire in the morning before he could talk to Kate.

At Gresham Abbey, Kate was still in a state of dismay regarding her anonymous letter, wondering if it were simply some nasty joke, or if its horrible suggestion about Rupert was true. But she was also beset with the issue of how to proceed with Mrs Priestley and Nanny.

If only Rupert were here to offer guidance. But she was on her own, and she simply had to do the best she could and hope that Rupert would approve. Of course, if what the note had said was true, he might not care much, one way or another.

With a heavy heart, she settled the children in one corner of the yellow drawing room with their toys, and rang for one of the housemaids, requesting that the two women in question should wait on her without delay.

They arrived, grim-faced and subdued. Kate did not ask them to sit down, even though she was aware that

Nanny, as an elderly lady with stiff joints, would have been more comfortable.

She began by tackling the house-keeper.

'Mrs Priestley,' she said. 'On the basis of what I discovered earlier, I made some accusations against you.'

'Yes, ma'am.'

'Were those accusations justified?'

The woman's lips tightened. 'I was intending to record the items in the accounts book, ma'am. But we have been busy in the last few days since the Earl returned and I had not got around to it. This kind of oversight has never happened before. And if you would just give me a chance, my lady, I promise you it will never happen again.'

Oh, my goodness, thought Kate, trying to untangle the ins and outs of this carefully rehearsed speech. Was Mrs Priestley both a thief and a liar? She suspected that this was the case. But she had no proof. And even if she were sure, then she still had to consider whether to show mercy, and give a thief a second chance. She also had to consider the danger of being taken for a ride. Moreover, how she dealt with this situation would set the pattern for years to come. If, indeed, there were going to be years to come. The words in the anonymous note kept ringing in her head, making her wretched.

She looked hard at Mrs Priestley, keeping her in suspense for a few moments longer.

'I am prepared to give you the benefit of the doubt,' she said at last.

'Oh, thank you, ma'am,' the house-keeper exclaimed. 'Will you be telling the Earl about this; my lady?' she asked hesitantly.

'I will have to think about that,' Kate answered. 'In the meantime, I would like to see the accounts book every morning. And I would also like to make it quite clear that I do not approve of members of staff drinking port during their working hours.'

Mrs Priestley blinked, her sturdy frame sagging with relief. 'Yes, ma'am.'

Kate now turned her attention to the nanny. Kindly, but firmly, she told the old lady that she thought it would be best for her to take a rest from her duties for the next few days. 'I shall make alternative arrangements for the children's care,' she said.

'I have been the nanny here for forty years,' the woman protested.

'Then maybe it is time to consider retiring,' Kate said softly.

Mixed emotions crossed the nanny's face.

'I will talk to the Earl,' Kate said, feeling quite out of her depth in making decisions about this woman who had presumably been like a second mother to Rupert. The one thing she did feel confident about was protecting his children from the woman's control and neglect.

When the nanny had made her slow, stiff exit, Kate sat back in her chair, her limbs shaking as though she had just climbed a high and challenging mountain. She prayed for Rupert to return.

She played with the children, ordered up tasty meals from the kitchen for them, and eventually put them to bed. But the hours passed, and there was no sign of him.

Midnight came and went, and Rupert still did not come. Kate could not help asking herself whether he was with some other love: a lady far more enchanting and worldly than herself? And if so, what she should do about it?

★ ★ ★

After a mainly sleepless night on a makeshift bed in the nursery, Kate woke early from a fitful doze and went in search of Bea, who had a pleasant little room overlooking the park at the back of Gresham Abbey. She found her maid already dressed, and tidying her room.

Bea had been deeply concerned to hear that her mistress had temporarily suspended the nanny from work. But being a practical girl, and conscious of her place in the scheme of things, she had kept her reservations private.

This morning, however, seeing Kate's exhausted, anxious face, she burst out, 'Oh, ma'am, did you have a wink of sleep last night?'

'Well, maybe a few winks,' Kate said, trying to sound positive. She had not told Bea of her intention to sleep near the children, and had climbed into bed as usual after dismissing her maid, then crept up to the nursery.

'Shall I bring breakfast?' Bea enquired.

'Yes. Just toast and coffee. And would you bring it up to the nursery, and also some food for the children? I'll eat my breakfast with them.'

'Very well,' Bea said, regarding her mistress with a worried frown.

Kate went back to the nursery and took the children from their cots. They were delighted to see her and instantly trotted off to find toys to bring for her inspection. Much as she enjoyed their company and was delighted to see how happy they were to be with someone

144

who would play and talk to them, she realised that she could not play the role of a nanny all the time. She had the overseeing of the house to consider, her role as the Countess of Gresham, and also, most importantly, her role as Rupert's wife.

She wondered if she had been over-impulsive in sending the old nanny away, without giving a thought to who else would take on the care of the children. She recalled that there had been a young nursemaid travelling with Nanny and the children on the train. Where was she now? How could Kate find out? The obvious person to ask in Rupert's absence was Mrs Priestley, but she felt a distinct disinclination to consult that particular lady.

Sighing, she looked out of the window, hoping with all her heart that Rupert might return very soon. And yet, all the time, she was thinking of the little note and its poisonous contents. *It is surely all nonsense,* she told herself. She was beginning to wonder if it had come from Lord Walton, whom she knew was annoyed at her rejection of his advances. That must surely be it. And if so, there was nothing to worry about. Even so . . .

After the children had finished their breakfasts, she took them to the yellow drawing room while she considered what was to be done with regard to the running of the house, and instructing the housekeeper and the cook.

Hedges came in with the morning post and the newspapers. Kate jumped up from the floor where she was helping the children to build a tower. She was suddenly conscious that her hair was not yet properly dressed and that her dress was crumpled — and, worse than that, spotted with scraps of boiled egg and buttery toast from the children's breakfast.

Smoothing her skirt, she bid Hedges a good morning. He nodded his acknowledgement, placed the post and papers on a table, then looked across to the children and slowly raised his eyebrows before departing.

Beginning to feel very harassed, Kate sorted through the envelopes, praying there would be no further unsigned messages for her, which was mercifully the case. There was, however, a letter for Rupert written in a flowery hand, almost certainly that of a woman.

Kate's heart gave little jumps of alarm as she handled the thick paper. And then she saw that it bore his sister Lady Helen's seal. *Stop it!* she told herself, horrified to find that she was turning into a suspicious wife. As she tried to calm her feelings she was aware of little Josefa trotting up to her knee. Looking up she saw that the child was carrying a large Chinese vase — one of a pair placed either side of the fireplace.

Involuntarily she gave a little cry of alarm. The child's face crumpled with dismay and before Kate could reassure her, she had dropped the vase onto the polished wood floorboards where it shattered into pieces.

Oh, heavens! 'It's all right, darling,'

she told Josefa, at the same time thinking of how valuable the vase must be. What on earth would Rupert think? It seemed to Kate that she was making blunders at every turn.

She rang the bell frantically for a housemaid and asked her to sweep up the china fragments and keep them in a safe place. Then she rang for Bea in the hope of restoring some order to her person and her state of mind. In twenty minutes, she was back in the yellow drawing room wearing an emerald silk dress and with her hair in a neatly plaited chignon. Little Josefa and Constance were washed, dressed and occupied with toys and books.

Then, suddenly, her heart leapt as she heard carriage wheels on the drive, and saw the dark red wheels and the gold Gresham crest glide into view. 'He is back,' she whispered in joy, all her doubts temporarily swept away.

She ran to the window, watching with eager anticipation as a footman stepped forward and opened the door of the carriage. However it was not Rupert who climbed out, but a small, plump man with wild, uncombed hair, bushy face whiskers, tiny wire-framed glasses and a long swirling cloak. He stood for a moment, looking up at Gresham Abbey with intense interest.

Kate felt a tremor of alarm, but was reassured when Rupert sprang from the carriage and beckoned the man to walk with him to the front door. Hedges came to meet them, and two footmen began unloading the luggage.

Soon there were voices in the great entrance hall, and suddenly Kate felt a wave of shyness wash over her at the thought of seeing her new husband again, and of the need to welcome an unknown guest. As she patted her hair and checked that her gown was free from the marks of sticky little fingers, Hedges knocked on the door, and slid himself inside, saying, 'Ma'am, the Earl has arrived back in the company of Mr Igor Voronsky.'

The plump man strode through the

door, walked straight up to Kate, and took both of her hands. 'Ah, the lovely Contessa! You are even more beautiful, my dear, than your worthy husband led me to believe.' He raised both of her hands to his lips and planted a large juicy kiss on each palm. Startled, Kate watched as he began to examine her fingers, spreading them out and running his own fingers up and down their length.

As Rupert walked through the door, her eyes sought his, asking silent questions about this strange, wild-looking visitor. Despite all her efforts to the contrary, she wondered once again about his fidelity. He smiled at her, making her heart sing as he came up close and dropped a light kiss on the top of her head. 'Kate, my dear, allow me to present Mr Igor Voronsky, the renowned violin virtuoso.'

Ah! Now she understood the reason for the visitor's interest in her hands. Although she had to admit that his continuing ferocious assessment of her person was somewhat unnerving.

Josefa and Constance, who had been playing quietly behind the sofa now came running to greet their father, having heard his voice. 'Papa, Papa!' they shouted, clutching at his legs.

Kate waited for Rupert to swing them up into his arms but instead he put a hand on each of their heads and gave them a little pat. And when his eyes connected with hers, she realised immediately that their presence here in the drawing room was not entirely to his liking. The flash of displeasure vanished almost instantly, but Kate felt almost as shocked and hurt as though Rupert had openly taken her to task on the matter.

'Such dear, sweet children!' Voronsky exclaimed, glancing at the two little girls for a fleeting moment before turning his attention back to Kate. 'And so, my dear, I have to tell you that your good husband and I met up by chance in Claridges yesterday and, can you believe it, we spent the evening talking about your promising talent on the violin. And I cannot wait to hear you play for my very own pleasure.'

'I see,' Kate responded, somewhat alarmed at the prospect of playing her violin under the scrutiny of this ebullient musician.

She noticed that Rupert had summoned Hedges and was having a few quiet words with him. The butler then stepped forward and offered to show Voronsky to his suite of rooms.

'We lunch in an hour,' Rupert told his guest. 'And after that I should be delighted to show you around Gresham Abbey and all its treasures.'

'What could be more agreeable?' Vorornsky exclaimed. 'Apart from hearing the dear Countess play her violin, of course.'

'I am sure she will be delighted to do so later on,' Rupert said, smoothly. He waited for the guest to leave the room and then turned to Kate. 'My dear, what are the children doing downstairs at this time of the day?'

'I am looking after them, for the time being,' Kate said, painfully aware that she had behaved in a way unacceptable in Rupert's eyes.

His gaze was cool and appraising. 'I see. And where is Nanny?'

'She is not well,' Kate told him, instantly regretting this deception and wondering how to put it right — and explain the situation without displeasing him further. 'I suggested that she rest at home for a few days.'

'I am sorry to hear she is indisposed,' Rupert said, his voice calm and formal. 'But there is no need for you to take on the role of nanny, there are a number of nursemaids who can be called upon in this kind of situation.'

'Yes, I am sorry. I didn't know quite who to call on,' Kate said, her eyes appealing to him.

He smiled. 'Of course not, my dear. How could I expect you to? And much of this is my own fault for being absent.'

He is so good and understanding, Kate thought, her heart twisting with love for him. *I have to tell him the simple truth. That is always the best policy.*

She began to frame a little speech in her head, but then when she looked across to the children she saw that they were standing close by and listening in to this little exchange between her and their father. They were only small, that was true, but they were well able to understand a good deal of everyday conversation. It would not be appropriate, or kind, to allow them to hear the discussion that would inevitably take place if she were to recount what had happened the day before with their elderly nanny.

Rupert was watching her, sensing her indecision. 'My dear,' he said, 'it is not appropriate for the Countess, my wife, to be a childminder. I am delighted that you are taking such a kind interest in my children, but it really will not do for you to be totally occupied in their care — even as a stopgap.'

'No, I do see that,' she said,

miserably. She was coming to understand how much she had to learn about being Rupert's wife. She had walked into this marriage with dazzled and half-closed eyes. She did not know him at all. And the idea of even thinking of asking him where he had been the day before and the afternoon before that, was simply unthinkable.

'The children's main residence at this stage in their life is in the nursery,' Rupert told her. 'They should only come down to the main reception rooms for an hour or so at tea-time.'

Kate tried not to look too shocked. She had been about to ask if that was what had happened when his previous wife was alive. But on reflection, she thought better of it. Maybe complete openness and honesty was not always the best policy in every tricky situation.

'That is the usual way in high-born families,' Rupert explained.

'Yes.' Kate swallowed hard. *This was not the way in my family,* she thought, sensing trouble ahead.

But for now she decided she must simply make a great effort to play her part as Rupert's new wife as best she could. Within the hour the nursemaid she had seen on the train miraculously appeared, and took the children away to the nursery. Rupert armed himself with the morning post and the newspapers and went to his room to wash and change after his train journey. In the dining room the servants set about laying the table for lunch. Domestic order was restored. But Kate felt herself beset with troubles.

7

Whilst Kate was wrestling with her problems, Arabella Cheveney was thinking constantly of Rupert and how to renew their liaison. She simply could not believe that he could just cut her out of his life.

She hated her humdrum life in the country. Mr Cheveney was perfectly content and not prepared to put up with the heat and dust of London during the hot months. All he wanted to do was potter about the estate, eat a good lunch and dinner and retire to the library with a bottle of port in the evenings. He no longer cared much for visiting or entertaining, and Arabella felt she would die of boredom and inertia. The renewing of her seduction of Rupert Gresham was the most enticing project she could think of.

She entertained herself by reflecting

on the fame and renown of beautiful, influential mistresses down the ages: Louis XV's Madame de Pompadour and King Charles II's Nell Gwynne. Remembering that Nell had been of low and common birth, she switched her thoughts to Barbara Villiers, an elegant lady who had produced a son for Charles, something his poor little wife had never managed.

She kept returning to her belief that Rupert simply could not live without her. She would not accept that a mere chit like Kate Roscoe could keep his interest. She was a north-country nobody, ignorant of the pleasures a real woman could give a man. Rupert was an experienced man of the world; Kate would never satisfy him fully. But how to get him back?

Sitting at the elegant writing desk in her boudoir she nibbled the end of her quill pen. On the desk top were several screwed-up pieces of paper, sweet little notes she had begun for his delight, then rejected as unsuitable. Grovelling was out of the question, but hectoring was not appropriate either.

Damn Rupert, she thought. *Damn my wretched husband and the horrid countryside and the dull old generals and farming gentry who live here. Damn wretched little Kate Roscoe. In fact, damn just about everything.* She laid her head on the desk and shed scalding tears of fury.

In time she sat up and pulled her shoulders back. She must not sit about moping, allowing fate to toy with her like some puppet. She must formulate plans. Thinking and writing were all very well. She must do something.

★   ★   ★

At lunch Igor Voronsky enjoyed himself immensely, putting away large quantities of food, and not stinting himself on partaking of the fine claret Rupert had asked Hedges to bring up from the cellar. Despite this enthusiastic fuelling of his hunger and thirst, he was still able to talk nonstop; regaling Rupert and Kate with stories of his triumphant performances in concert halls and aristocratic salons throughout Europe.

Kate found herself both amused and alarmed by this theatrical display, remembering that she would be obliged to perform on the violin herself in due course. She wondered how well Rupert knew the great virtuoso. Voronsky did not strike her as the sort of man Rupert would choose to spend time with. But glancing at her husband, she found it hard to work out what his thoughts were: his face was pleasantly impassive.

How little I know about him, she thought, longing to be alone with him once again, to feel his lean body against hers — if he still desired her.

She would have been surprised to discover that Rupert was not thinking of Voronsky at all. His mind was occupied with the issue of Lord Walton's threat to publish details of his personal affairs to the national press. So far nothing of that kind had appeared in print. He could only assume that Walton's proclamation had been mere bragging and bravado — he probably had little sway with the editor of *The Times*, or any other newspaper. And it was unlikely that his father would help him further his spiteful plots. So hopefully matters would rest there. Please God, that was the case.

When lunch was over it was agreed that Kate and Voronsky would meet at three o'clock in the main drawing room, where she would play her violin for his appreciation. She spent the intervening time practising. But her heart was not in her playing. Following the events of the last twenty-four hours, she found herself weary from lack of sleep and the anxiety of her new duties as mistress of Gresham Abbey. She worried about the children's welfare, wishing there would soon be an opportunity to speak to Rupert in private to share her feelings with him and tell him honestly about the unfortunate affair with the old nanny. And maybe she could even show him the detestable anonymous note. But, whilst pleasant and gentle in his manner towards her, Rupert was as aloof and inscrutable as ever, slipping away to speak to his estates manager, or simply to be on his own in the library.

Voronsky was seated at the grand piano in the corner of the drawing room when she entered, holding her violin and bow.

He swung around to greet her. 'Ah — my dear Countess! Stand beside me. Let us play together. What piece have you chosen to delight me with?'

Kate felt decidedly uneasy as she laid her chosen music on the piano. Voronsky glanced at it. 'Ah, the Bach partitas. An excellent choice.' He gave her an A on the piano and she set about tuning her instrument.

As she did so, the door opened softly and Rupert walked in, settling himself on one of the ornate chairs placed against the wall. Her mouth dried.

It was one thing playing for Voronsky, of whom she had a rather low opinion, despite his fame and talent. But she hated the idea of showing herself up in front of Rupert when he had made this effort to give her the chance of being assessed by a world famous musician. But she knew she was not going to show herself at her best this afternoon. She was too tired, too concerned about other matters, and sensed that she had been driven into a corner to undergo this test of her skill.

She took up her bow. Her hands were trembling so much she wondered if she would be able to play at all. But somehow the notes sang out.

After a few moments Voronsky stopped her. 'Quite nice, dear Countess,' he said. 'But there is too much tightness in your arms and fingers. You must relax. You must breathe deeply. Come, take some deep, deep breaths.'

Kate felt there was no alternative but to stand there, huffing and puffing.

'Good, good! Now begin again!' Voronsky commanded.

Unnerved now, Kate struggled through

the piece. Voronsky closed his eyes nodding in time to the music. At the close of the piece he opened them again and gave a long sigh. 'Quite nice playing,' he said. 'A nice tone, as well.' He then took his own violin from its case. 'Now I shall play for you,' he said, with a smug smile.

Kate knew that he was damning her with faint praise. She felt inadequate and disappointed, sensations she had never experienced before when playing her beloved violin. She wished Voronsky were miles away and had never appeared in her life. She had no ambitions regarding her violin; she merely liked playing it for her own entertainment and for her family. Glancing at Rupert, she felt a flare of anger towards him for setting up this whole humiliating scenario. But instantly she relented, knowing his intention had been kind, to encourage her in her artistic achievements.

Suddenly utterly drained, she excused herself to Voronsky and made for the door. She felt Rupert's eyes on her, but could not bring herself to meet his gaze. She went to her room and lay down on the bed. She wished and wished that Rupert would come to find her. But that did not happen, and eventually she drifted into an uneasy sleep.

★   ★   ★

Whilst Kate was dining with Rupert and his guest, Arabella was lunching with her husband, who was mainly silent, his mind occupied with what he might discuss with the head gardener that afternoon. Arabella was irritated by his lack of conversation, although she would have been equally annoyed had he held forth on the prosaic matters that usually interested him. She took a long sip of the fine Vouvray wine from his cellar, which was at least one thing she could enjoy.

'We are invited to dine at the Longstaffs' this evening,' he suddenly announced, putting down his fork.

'You never told me about this!'

Arabella protested.

Mr Cheveney looked chastened. 'I'm very sorry, my love. Celia Longstaff sent an invitation round yesterday afternoon. I forgot to mention it.'

Arabella did not find the elderly Longstaff couple particularly good company, but recalling that their house was very close to Gresham Abbey, her interest sharpened. 'Very well, my dear.' She smiled brightly at her husband, her mind filling with possible new schemes. She had not yet come up with a satisfactory stratagem to get her lover back, but now, with the chance of being so close to Gresham Abbey having fallen into her lap like a gift from heaven, she knew it was imperative she use the opportunity.

She pushed her raspberries around her plate until they were nothing more than a bright red pool. But inspiration refused to come, and frustration settled around her like a grey cloak. Looking idly down the table, she noticed that the silver rose bowl in the centre was tarnished around the rim and that she would have to speak with the house-keeper about it. And whilst her conscious thoughts were engaged in that plan, so another plan freed itself from the cage of her unconscious, providing her with a perfect reason to visit Gresham Abbey and see her darling once more.

She gave a little laugh of delight. Her husband looked up. 'Gerald, my love,' she told him fondly, 'I think that visiting the Longstaffs tonight is a splendid idea.'

★　★　★

Rupert had been relieved when, shortly after Kate's brief recital, Igor Voronsky announced his intention of returning to London on the evening train. Rupert was aware that his invitation to the great violinist had been a sorry mistake. The man was clearly extremely vain, utterly taken up with his own self-importance. Poor Kate had been put through unnecessary stress and made to feel worthless as a musician, which was grossly unfair. In fact, each time he ran over the scene in the drawing room he felt more angry.

Deciding that Voronsky was capricious and volatile, he was eager to get rid of him as soon as possible in case he changed his mind and stayed on to swill down more claret. He ordered the carriage to be brought round without delay and undertook to personally supervise the guest's swift departure from Gresham Abbey and his safe boarding of the train at the station.

Arabella had dressed with great care for the visit to the Longstaffs. She had also unearthed from the store of house silver a loving cup that had belonged to a long-dead relative, had one of the housemaids polish it and wrapped it in tissue paper. She slipped in a little note addressed to the Earl and the new Countess, as a gesture of her affection for them.

'Is this wise, my dear?' her husband enquired, when she announced her wish for the carriage to drop him off at the Longstaffs whilst she went on to make a brief visit to Gresham Abbey to deliver the gift. 'The Earl and Countess might be engaged with other, important business.'

'I do not intend to intrude, and I shall not be staying more than a few minutes,' she told him, firmly.

Arabella had never been sure exactly how much her husband knew of her relationship with Rupert Gresham, though she suspected he must have some idea. She guessed that like many rather dull, elderly husbands he would not be too unhappy, even if he knew the truth. To have a beautiful young wife charming enough to attract the attention of an aristocrat was something of a feather in an old man's cap.

As Gresham Abbey came into view, beautiful and dignified in the evening sunshine, Arabella's heart beat fast. When the Earl saw her alongside the dull little Countess, he would realise what a mistake he had made, and she, Arabella, would have him back in her bed. She took another sip from the flask stored in her reticule. Brandy always made her feel gloriously daring.

Inside the Abbey, Hedges was crossing the hallway when he noticed a fine carriage approaching. He summoned a footman to meet the visitors. Watching as Arabella Cheveney was handed down from the carriage, he felt a bolt of irritation. That wretched woman — what did she mean by coming here? Could he get rid of her before the Countess had any knowledge of what would obviously be an unwelcome visit?

Unfortunately the Countess chose that moment to emerge from her room. She had just reached the bottom of the staircase when Arabella stepped through the door, handing her visiting card to Hedges.

'Earl Gresham is not at home, ma'am,' Hedges said, his face stony.

Arabella blinked. 'Oh! I see.' Peering around him, she smiled sweetly at Kate, then swept forward, extending her hand. 'My dear Countess Gresham, allow me to introduce myself. I am Mrs Gerald Cheveney. My husband and I are neighbours of yours, and great friends of the Earl.'

The greeting was innocent enough, but with a female's instinct Kate knew instantly that this woman had had some kind of relationship with Rupert in the past. She recalled Lord Walton's remark at Mrs Follett's ball about Rupert's having a 'reputation'. But then he had been a widower, and it was not unusual for liaisons to be made at such times. For men, at any rate. Even so, she felt decidedly unhappy about this lady's arrival.

'Please go through into the drawing room,' she told Mrs Cheveney. She then turned to Hedges. 'Where is the Earl?'

'His Lordship has taken Mr Voronsky to the station, ma'am,' Hedges told her. 'I would imagine that he will not be back for an hour or so. He asked me to assure you he would return as soon as possible.'

Voronsky gone! *Well, that is a relief,* thought Kate. Now she just had to deal with the alarmingly beautiful Mrs Cheveney.

Walking into the drawing room, she found that lady gazing at the portrait of Rupert's father which hung over the marble fireplace.

'Please forgive me for intruding,' Mrs Cheveney said, turning around and opening her blue eyes wide. 'I have brought you and Rupert a little gift.'

'That is very kind,' Kate said, keeping her voice steady. 'Do please sit down, Mrs Cheveney.'

The older woman looked at Kate with a fixed smile, making no effort to disguise her interest in the young Countess's face and figure. But her feelings were hard for Kate to read. 'Thank you, my dear Countess,' Mrs Cheveney said in honeyed tones. 'But I shall not stay. My husband and I have a dinner engagement. We must not be late.'

Kate smiled graciously, heartily pleased to hear that the visitor would soon be departing. 'I shall tell Earl Gresham you called when he returns.'

'Dear Rupert, he has so many obligations to fulfil,' Mrs Cheveney observed. 'I expect you hardly see him at all?'

'On the contrary,' Kate said, sensing that the two of them were engaging in a velvet-gloved skirmish, 'we spend a good deal of time together.'

'Really! I am so pleased to hear that. Rupert had some dreadfully lonely months after his first wife died.' She slanted a glance at Kate, who felt her stomach lurch at the clear implication that Rupert had only been lonely until Mrs Cheveney appeared in his life. She considered this a very superficial way of looking at Rupert's past loss and his grieving. One thing she had learned about her husband was that he was a very complex man.

'I hear that you are not going on a honeymoon journey,' Mrs Cheveney remarked casually, although her eyes glittered like rapiers.

Kate gave a start. How could Mrs Cheveney possibly know about that?

'Rupert told me so when he came to visit me a day or two ago,' Mrs Cheveney explained. 'We spent a most amusing afternoon together.' She shot Kate a smile of undisguised triumph.

Pain and shock at what she was implying tore through Kate like a hot knife and she was unable to make any reply. She also realised that Arabella was the author of the poisonous letter — and not a person to be trifled with.

Arabella gave a serene smile. Seeing that her dart had struck home, she picked up her reticule and made for the door.

As she reached the hallway, Hedges glided forward to usher the visitor out. Kate heard her voice ring out with the words, 'Good evening.'

She stood in the drawing room, stunned with the news that Rupert had made contact with his mistress since their marriage. Scenes rose into her mind; hateful and insistent. The idea of her darling Rupert holding Arabella Cheveney in his arms was so hurtful that she cried out. Then she thought of Rupert's visits to her own bed in the night, and she knew she could not receive him tonight with love and honesty following Arabella's insinuations. In fact there was no possibility she could stay at Gresham Abbey and confront him at all whilst holding all this dread and suspicion in her heart.

★ ★ ★

Instead of returning to her carriage, Arabella walked around the west wing of the Abbey and leaned against the stones of the great house. Her head swirled from the brandy she had consumed and tears of anger and frustration pricked behind her eyes. Whilst she had stirred up a hornet's nest for the Countess, she had not seen Rupert and was not at all certain of ever getting him back.

She was filled with a white-hot rage at him for throwing her over and installing a nonentity in his splendid family home. Oh yes, it had been good to tease and humiliate the new Countess, but that was not enough to calm her raging jealousy. She felt herself fuelled with savagery for her former lover. If he were to suddenly appear, she truly believed she would kill him.

Gazing across to the rose garden, she saw a nursemaid leading Rupert's two children towards the west door. She supposed they had been out for a breath of air. Such sweet little things, so fresh and new, so vulnerable.

The little group had just disappeared into the house when one of the children came back out, clearly looking for a lost toy. Arabella watched, her heart pounding with emotion. But no one came for the child, who continued trotting about, scanning the ground. Plans sprang like magic into Arabella's mind. Oh, how sweet it would be to hurt Rupert, wound him more deeply than any other blow she could think of inflicting.

Spotting a doll lying on the gravel near the house, she walked forward, her smile gentle and encouraging. 'Here is your doll, darling,' she said, picking up the toy and handing it to the child. 'Shall I take you back to your nurse? Or would you like to see my lovely horses?'

Her tones were so honeyed, her smile so sweet, the little girl put her hand up to be held and the two of them walked towards Arabella's carriage.

*   *   *

Kate paced the drawing room, wondering what she should do. In time she heard Arabella's carriage rumble away and closed her eyes at the horror of thinking yet again of that lady resting in the curve of Rupert's arms. Impulsively she wrote him a note, simply saying she was going to visit her mother for a few days. She tucked it into the sleeve of her gown, planning to leave it on a silver tray in the hallway and then ask Hedges to send to the stables for one of the smaller carriages to take her to the station. But she knew she could not leave without saying goodbye to the children.

As she made her way to the nursery wing, the newly appointed young nanny came running down the corridor, crying out in distress.

'Oh, ma'am, it's little Lady Josefa!' she exclaimed. 'I cannot find her!' She stared at Kate, terror and panic in her eyes.

Kate, while alarmed, knew that children could easily wander off and get lost in a house of this size. 'Where did you last see her?' she asked.

'In the rose garden, ma'am. I was letting the children play outside before giving them their bedtime milk. I thought they had both followed me inside, but after a time I noticed that Lady Josefa was missing. I went straight back out but she was nowhere to be seen. And she is not in the nursery. Oh, my Lady Countess, where can she have gone?'

'I shall ask Hedges to send the servants to make a full search of the house and the garden,' Kate said, trying to stay calm. 'Is Lady Constance in the nursery?'

'Yes. She is drinking her milk. She is very tired.'

'Go and look after her,' Kate said. 'I'm sure we shall find Lady Josefa.'

Ten minutes went by, but even with all the servants searching for her, the little girl was nowhere to be seen.

Kate went to find Hedges, but he was out with the others. She went to the stables and asked one of the grooms to saddle up a pony for her. 'I am going to search beyond the grounds,' she told the young man, swinging up into the saddle and putting the pony into a canter.

She was a good horsewoman and soon had the measure of the pony, which was spirited but biddable. She tried to think what could have happened to Josefa, but her mind refused to work, she was now so desperately worried. She recalled newspaper reports of children who had been taken, and huge ransoms demanded, and her blood ran cold.

After ten minutes of spirited cantering, she saw a carriage approaching. It bore the Gresham crest; it would be Rupert returning from the station. She waved to the coachman to stop, her heart beating hard.

Rupert swung himself from the coach and strode across to the pony. 'Kate! Whatever are you doing, my dear? Don't tell me you are running away from me already?' His eyes crinkled with amusement as he looked up at her. And then he saw the strain on her face and his own features stilled. 'What is it? What is the matter?'

'Oh, Rupert,' she burst out, 'little Josefa has gone missing!'

'Dear God! Tell me exactly what you know.'

Kate did her best to explain, though she could hardly speak. At the end of her account, he looked hard at her. 'Anything else? Kate!' he warned when she stayed silent. 'Tell me what you are hiding.'

'A lady called Mrs Cheveney came to visit a little while ago.'

He froze. 'Be damned, she did. And no doubt it is she who has taken my little girl.' Desperation and fear stretched his features.

Kate gasped, suddenly understanding what must have happened, and just how dangerous Arabella Cheveney was. She stared at him. 'Do you know where she might have gone with Josefa?'

He frowned in thought. 'I believe I do — and that is where we shall go, without delay.' He called to the coachman and asked him to uncouple one of the carriage horses. 'Leave his bridle on,' he told the man. Swinging himself up onto the horse's bare back, he directed Kate to bring her pony alongside. 'Keep close to me,' he said, as they all set off at a furious pace.

'Rupert, where are we going?' Kate asked, breathless as her pony went into a furious gallop. 'How long will it take?'

'About fifteen minutes. We're making for Mrs Cheveney's childhood home. It is empty now, but she still uses it on occasions.'

No doubt to entertain her lovers, thought Kate bitterly.

'We need to get there as soon as possible,' he said, his breath coming fast. 'She can be wild and unpredictable when crossed. I paid her a visit a couple of days ago and made it plain that she has no place in my life now. She will be trying to get back at me.'

So Mrs Cheveney has been lying, Kate thought, understanding all she needed to. Rupert had been true to his wife. She reached across and pressed her hand on his. Thank God she hadn't run off back to her mother. How could she ever have doubted him?

'We will find Josefa,' she told Rupert firmly. 'She will be safe.' She prayed more fervently for it than for anything in her life before.

8

Arabella did not know what to do to stop the child crying. She had no experience whatever of young children. She rocked the child on her knee, but nothing calmed its sobs. Soon her dress was wet with the child's tears and running nose. The cries were grating on her nerves like scalding needles piercing her. She longed to sleep. How did nursemaids manage when children behaved like this? Could it go on for hours? Days? She recalled stories of low women battering their young children, killing them, even. Suddenly it was possible to comprehend.

She carried the child into an ante-room, laid her on a sofa and shut the door on her sobs. She went to the drawing room, but the cries went on.

★ ★ ★

Rupert turned his horse into some fine ornate gates and let the reins go slack. Kate slowed her courageous, now exhausted pony to a walk. Looking ahead she saw a gracious house built of pink brick. The front door was half open and fresh traces of carriage wheels marked the gravel drive.

Rupert rode up to the door, jumped off his horse and helped Kate dismount. 'I think it would best if you were to stay out of sight until I call for you,' he told her. He squeezed her hand and then moved forward.

'Hullo, there!' he called out. 'Is anyone about?' There was an ominous silence in the house and his blood ran cold. 'Hullo! Hullo!'

A door opened and Arabella came out, her eyes both fierce and terrified. In her hand was the small rapier she always carried in her reticule.

Rupert walked slowly forward, assessing Arabella's mood. He saw the glint of steel in her hand. The silence was like a foretelling of doom.

He thought it best to deal with his wild-looking mistress as gently as possible. Very slowly he held out his arms. 'My dear,' he said. 'I shall take care of everything now. Mmm?'

Arabella's glance was like the flick of a snake's tongue. She moved forward, then suddenly, hearing a sound, spun around and leapt at Kate who had moved to stand in the doorway. She was much taller than Kate and instantly had her in her grasp, one arm thrown around her neck, the other hand pressing the tip of her rapier into the skin of Kate's throat.

'Arabella,' Rupert said softly, 'put the rapier down. Then we can talk about what it is that you want from me.'

Arabella's eyes gleamed in the half light. 'I want to hurt you, Rupert,' she said with icy conviction. 'I want to hurt you and your wife.'

Rupert saw the demon glinting in her eyes and understood that at this moment, Arabella was probably more mad than bad. His mind sought ways of getting through this terrible impasse. And terror clawed at him as he feared for Kate and wondered about the fate of his little girl.

He made himself speak calmly. 'No, you don't want to hurt my wife, or my child. Just let Kate go, and then bring me my little girl. After that, you can do whatever you wish with me.'

Arabella gave a snort of derision and pressed the tip of the rapier a little harder on Kate's skin. 'You're hurting me, Arabella,' Kate said, following Rupert's lead of outward calmness.

Arabella relaxed the pressure a little. 'You're of no account,' she told Kate. 'It is him I wish to hurt.' She glared at Rupert. 'This man who has thrown me over and condemned me to a life of dreariness and boredom.'

'Very well,' Rupert said. 'So all you have to do is free Kate and bring me my little girl. Then you may cut me to pieces, if you wish.' He loosened his cravat and showed her his throat.

'Where is little Josefa?' Kate asked,

trying to sound gentle, whilst still conscious of the knife at her throat.

A ghastly silence followed. Kate saw that Rupert's face was a white mask of agony for the safety and fate of his child. Arabella stared in hatred at him. Then suddenly she tightened her grip on Kate, so that she cried out.

Rupert found himself standing frozen and useless as seconds passed. He tried to judge how long it would take to move forward and spring on Arabella. Too long to be confident that Kate would not be hurt.

From outside came the sound of wheels, then footsteps and a man's voice. 'Arabella. Are you there? What is happening?'

Gerald Cheveney appeared in the doorway. The blood left his face. 'Arabella, what are you doing?

'Go away,' Arabella told him dismissively.

Cheveney stepped forward and, mild though he was, his presence altered the charged dynamic between the tense trio of a man, his wife and his former lover. Arabella suddenly pressed the rapier so hard it cut Kate's skin, and as she let out a howl of terror Rupert took his chance to spring forward. In a voice of massive authority, he shouted to Arabella to drop the rapier and instinctively she did as he told her, at the same time letting Kate go and pushing her forward so that she stumbled onto the floor.

Rupert propelled Arabella into her husband's arms, then turned to Kate. As he helped her up, there came the muffled scream of a terrified infant.

Rupert closed his eyes, thanking God that she was alive. He took Kate's hand and the two of them hurried forward to find the little girl. Following the cries Rupert eventually pulled open a door and saw his darling Josefa; a poor, deserted figure bellowing in despair and misery as she lay deserted and frightened on the floor.

He scooped her up and held her close. For a few moments she was bewildered, and then she flung her chubby arms around his neck. 'Papa!'

Kate knelt beside them and Rupert wrapped an arm around each of them, his little girl and his beloved new wife, hugging them close.

When they returned to the hallway, they found Gerald Cheveney keeping guard by his wife, who was now slumped in a chair, exhausted and spent.

'Is all well with the little girl?' Gerald asked anxiously. Rupert nodded.

'My coachman came to tell me what had happened,' he explained. 'Arabella had commanded him to drive here from Gresham with the child. The poor man did the best he could in the circumstances.' He looked sadly at his crumpled, tear-stained wife. 'I am so sorry for all the trouble she has caused.' He looked up at Rupert, standing solemn and silent with Josefa in his arms. 'Will you be involving the police?' he enquired sadly.

'No,' Rupert said. 'But you will take care of her, won't you, Gerald?'

His words conveyed both a well-meant

request, and a warning.

'Of course,' Gerald answered.

Kate found herself impressed with the elderly banker. He might not be the most exciting of men, but he was clearly one of both integrity and stoicism. Arabella was lucky to have him.

★   ★   ★

The next morning Rupert and Kate sat side by side in the nursery at Gresham Abbey and smiled at each other like children on Christmas morning. In the bedroom beyond, the two children were sleeping peacefully.

'Little Josefa is doing so well after her ordeal,' Kate whispered.

'Yes.' He put his arm around her. 'And what about you and me, Kate?'

She saw the love shining from his eyes, and knew it was a strong, genuine love which, like hers, would grow and deepen over the years.

'We are going to be the happiest couple in all England,' she said, smiling with a hint of mischief.

His face became serious again. 'I am so very sorry you had to undergo all that distress from Arabella.'

'After she had spoken to me, I had actually wondered about running away as you suggested,' Kate said, slicing a wicked glance at him.

'You would never do that — would you?' he asked, raising his eyebrows.

'No. Or if I thought about it, I should wait to consult you first!'

'In the future we will talk about things.' His eyes had recovered their sardonic glint.

'Oh, most certainly. Especially regarding my views on the care of little children,' Kate said, slanting him another meaningful look.

He pulled her onto his knee. A few delicious moments passed.

'By the way,' he said, 'I intend to speak to my old nanny and give her a generous sum for her retirement.'

'I am glad,' Kate said, smiling to herself.

'And when I was in the hallway

earlier, I overheard Hedges telling Mrs Priestley that the Earl of Gresham's bride was a most courageous lady to ride off on a pony to look for a lost child. And Mrs Priestley told him she thought the Countess was a very fair and efficient mistress.' He gave Kate a quizzical glance. 'You have made quite an impression, Kate.'

I wonder what he would think if he knew the whole of it, Kate wondered. But she understood now that a good and wise Countess makes it her life's work to adore her husband and children, and to allow certain other matters to be addressed without troubling her loved ones.

She and Rupert spent most of the day with the children. And when the little ones were again asleep, they walked out into the park amongst the deer and sheep. They linked hands and Kate laid her head on Rupert's shoulder. As they made their way over the soft grass, the lamps which had been lit in Gresham Abbey glowed through the deepening dusk.

WILD FOR LOVE

Carol MacLean

Polly is an ecologist, passionate and uncompromising about wildlife rights. Against all her principles she falls in love with Jake, heir to a London media empire, whose development company is about to destroy a beautiful marsh. But can love ever blossom between two such different people? As Polly battles to save the marsh and learns to compromise for love, Jake finally finds the life he has always desired . . .

We do hope that you have enjoyed reading this large print book.

Did you know that all of our titles are available for purchase?

We publish a wide range of high quality large print books including:
Romances, Mysteries, Classics
General Fiction
Non Fiction and Westerns

Special interest titles available in large print are:
The Little Oxford Dictionary
Music Book, Song Book
Hymn Book, Service Book

Also available from us courtesy of Oxford University Press:
Young Readers' Dictionary
(large print edition)
Young Readers' Thesaurus
(large print edition)

For further information or a free brochure, please contact us at:
Ulverscroft Large Print Books Ltd.,
The Green, Bradgate Road, Anstey,
Leicester, LE7 7FU, England.
Tel: (00 44) **0116 236 4325**
Fax: (00 44) **0116 234 0205**